Agent Starling: Operation Baked Beans
An original concept by author Jenny Moore
© Jenny Moore

Cover artwork by Lee Cosgrove

Published by MAVERICK ARTS PUBLISHING LTD
Studio 11, City Business Centre, 6 Brighton Road,
Horsham, West Sussex, RH13 5BB
+44 (0) 1403 256941
© Maverick Arts Publishing Limited October 2019

A CIP catalogue record for this book is available
at the British Library.

ISBN: 978-1-84886-486-3

AGENT STARLING
OPERATION BAKED BEANS

JENNY MOORE

For Lucy, Daniel and Dafydd, with love

CHAPTER I

Oliver Starling was in the bath, washing jelly and custard out of his hair, when the greatest adventure of his life came calling.

It had been a pretty normal sort of morning until then, apart from the unfortunate incident with a runaway hamster and a flying bowl of trifle. In fact, it had been a pretty normal sort of *life* until then. Like most eleven-year-old boys, Oliver had never eaten a honey-coated dormouse or fought in an amphitheatre. He'd never been chased through the streets by angry Roman guards, and he'd never even heard of Dr Midnight, the world's number one evil genius. But all that was about to change.

"Oliver!" called his mum, from the hallway. He couldn't decide if she sounded excited or cross or just plain squeaky. Perhaps she'd spotted the custard splatters on her new curtains.

"Oliver!" she called again as she came charging up the stairs. "Come on, out you get, quick as you can." Her voice grew squeakier with every step. By the time she reached the bathroom door, she sounded like a cat with a trodden-on tail. "Get out! Get out! Get out!"

Oliver dunked his head under the water for custard-busting luck, then climbed out of the bath, wondering what all the fuss was about. Perhaps the Queen was on television again. Mrs Starling was potty about the royal family – totally and utterly bonkers. Not only did she stand and salute during the national anthem, she curtseyed every time she saw a first class stamp.

"What's going on?" he asked, shivering in his towel as Mrs Starling came tearing into the bathroom. She thrust a pile of clothes into his arms

– his 'best' clothes by the looks of it – and began combing his wet hair with her fingers. "And what's happened to my school uniform?" None of this was making any sense.

"Oh Oliver," his mum squealed, fishing a stray blob of jelly out of his fringe, "there's someone important here to see you. Someone *really* important." Her face was flushed with excitement, her bottom lip trembling like an over-excited slug. "He says he's here on the *Queen's* business," she added, attacking Oliver's chin with her royal wedding handkerchief and an extra-large helping of Mum-spit, "so I asked him to wait in the lounge while I came to fetch you."

"And I asked him to go away and let me eat my breakfast in peace," muttered Oliver's dad, appearing in the doorway behind her. "But no one ever listens to me."

Mrs Starling spun round with a face like thunder. "What are you doing up here?!" she shrieked at her husband. "You're supposed to be keeping him

9

entertained!"

'Entertaining' wasn't one of Mr Starling's strong points, unfortunately. Oliver must have heard his joke about the one-legged duck with a welly on his head about ten million times by now – and it never got any funnier. As for his idea of interesting conversation… he seemed to think people *wanted* to hear about his infected toenail. And that was on a good day. On a bad day, he'd probably get it out to show them.

"I can't be expected to entertain on an empty stomach," Mr Starling grumbled, scratching at his toe through a hole in his sock. "I haven't even finished my morning coffee yet."

"Why are you still here?" hissed his wife. "Go and make him a cup of tea or something."

Mr Starling stomped off to look after their mystery guest, muttering something about weirdos in funny coats and fake beards.

"Right," said Mrs Starling, giving Oliver's mouth one last rub with the slobbery hankie. "Into your clothes as quick as you can and mind your pleases and thank yous. And remember, don't say 'what', say 'pardon'." She glanced down at her own nightie and dressing gown. "Goodness gracious, I'd better get changed as well. Whatever will the Queen think when she hears I was still in my nightclothes? Oh, the shame of it all…" And with that she went haring off to her bedroom to slip into something more royally correct.

Oliver threw on his clothes and headed downstairs, closely followed by Mrs Starling, now dressed in her favourite Buckingham Palace sweatshirt… and a tiara. She had a string of Union Jack bunting wrapped round her neck like a scarf, and hand-knitted corgi slippers on her feet.

"Hurry up now," she said, pushing him through the lounge door, "you mustn't keep him waiting."

"Ah, there you are, Oliver," said Mr Starling, pulling his sock back on over his infected toenail. "If anyone wants me, I'll be in the kitchen, finishing my cold coffee." He hurried off, leaving Oliver alone with their strange visitor. He was dressed in an ankle-length raincoat, with dark glasses perched on top of a long pointed nose and a curly grey beard that kept slipping down his chin.

"Take a seat," said the man. "You're probably wondering why I'm here."

"Yes," agreed Oliver, popping a bubble of bath water in his left ear. That was *one* of the things he was wondering, along with 'Who are you?', 'Is this all a dream?' and 'Why are you wearing that ridiculous beard?' It looked like something out of the drama dressing-up box at school – like a bedraggled pirate crossed with a goat. "Please, thank you," he added for good measure, remembering his mum's instructions.

"The name's Owl," said the man, handing Oliver a royal blue business card with 'Agent Owl – *on her Majesty's S Service*' printed in bright white ink. "The *S* stands for 'Secret'," he whispered, tapping his nose and winking, "but keep that to yourself, eh? You never know *who* might be listening." He checked the curtains and cupboards for lurking eavesdroppers, muttering under his breath as he peered underneath the sofa and chairs. "We can't be too careful. His spies are everywhere."

"Whose pies?" asked Oliver, popping a bubble of bathwater in his right ear to cover his confusion. What sort of person hid pastry treats under the furniture?

"No," hissed Owl. "Not pies. *Spies*. They work for Dr Midnight, the world's number one evil genius. Chances are they're watching us even as we speak." He crossed back to the window and peered out. "There," he said, pointing to Number 47, where someone was peeping through the net curtains. "What did I tell you?"

"No. That's just old Mrs Peeker," said Oliver. "She's a bit on the nosy side, and her cat wees on everyone's shoes, but I'm sure she's not a spy."

"Ha! Don't be so sure. Dr Midnight's got plenty of old ladies working for him, you know. They're cheap labour and no one ever suspects them. Plus, they're good at knitting jackets for his pet poodle, Josephine." Owl shuddered. "You'll have to watch out for Josephine – she's got very sharp teeth."

"What?" said Oliver. "I mean, pardon?"

"Woolly jackets," repeated Owl, "and sharp teeth. But we haven't got time to worry about that now. We're looking for someone to undertake a top-secret mission, Oliver Starling, and our sources tell us you'd be perfect."

"Me?"

"Precisely. We heard you got a merit award for your school project on Roman Britain last term, and your great-great-great-great-more-greats-than-we've-got-time-for-great-grandfather was none other than Titus Stabbicus, the great centurion."

"Really?" Oliver straightened up in his seat.

"Agent B will fill you in on the details of the mission once we get to S Service Headquarters. All I need to know now is whether you're ready for the greatest adventure of your life?"

Oliver thought for a moment. Greatest adventure

ever or another day at school? It was a tough one.

"But what about breakfast? And what about Mum and Dad? They might not want me battling evil geniuses. Especially not on a weekday."

"Don't you worry about that," said Owl, readjusting his beard. "I'll have a word with them now." He fished around in the pockets of his raincoat and pulled out a large bar of chocolate. "This should keep you going for a bit."

Oliver got to work on the chocolate while Agent Owl got to work on his parents.

"I don't think so," he heard his mum say. "He's far too young for that sort of thing. Besides, I don't want him missing out on his education."

"But he wouldn't have to," Owl told her. "We'll be back before you know it."

"It's not every day someone in our family gets to do something exciting," Mr Starling said. "*I* haven't done anything exciting in twenty-six years."

"Do be quiet, dear."

"And, of course, the Queen will be able to thank

you in person at the next royal party," Owl added. "All our agents and their families are invited."

Mrs Starling gasped. "The *Queen*?" she squeaked. "In *person*, did you say? Well, I suppose *someone* needs to save the world from evil geniuses. After all, it's not every day a Starling gets to do something this exciting."

"That's what I said," grumbled Mr Starling, but no one was listening.

CHAPTER II

Ten minutes later, dressed in a matching raincoat and dark glasses (but without the pirate goat beard, thank goodness), Oliver followed Owl outside.

"Wow!" he gasped, admiring the sleek car waiting for them in the middle of the road. It looked like something out of a film, with built-in water-blasters, blacked-out windows and a silver question mark on the bonnet. Wait until he told Florence about *this!*

Oliver and Florence had been best friends since their first day at infant school, when Florence tripped over Oliver's lunchbox. She could be a bit clumsy like that sometimes, but she was also funny, daring and clever – very clever – and there was nothing she liked more than a good spy adventure story. And now Oliver was off on the start of his *own* spy adventure story. Oh no, but wait, secret agents were supposed to keep things secret, weren't they? Not that she'd have believed him anyway – Oliver could hardly believe it himself.

He felt super important as he climbed in, wearing his new outfit – like a proper spy. There wasn't much to spy just yet though, only Mrs Peeker peeking out from behind her net curtains as they whizzed off along Sherlock Avenue. In fact, it was hard to see much at all behind dark windows *and* dark glasses.

"Can I take these off now?" asked Oliver, squinting in the gloom.

"What?" Owl stared at him in disbelief, his mouth flapping open like a startled goldfish.

"My sunglasses, I mean," Oliver added, in case he thought he meant his shoes and socks. Perhaps Owl was still traumatized by his close-up with Mr

Starling's infected toe.

"Take off your glasses? Well, I don't know… I mean they're standard S Service uniform. I never take mine off. Never."

"What, not even at night?" asked Oliver. "Not even in the bath?"

Owl shook his head. "Of course not… although it does make finding the soap a bit difficult."

"How about if I promise to put them back on when we get there?" Oliver suggested, wishing he knew where 'there' was.

"Hmm. It's highly irregular," said Owl, "but I suppose so, if you insist…"

Oliver tucked his glasses into his raincoat pocket and pressed his nose up against the window, watching the houses and trees whoosh past. Every time they passed an old lady with a shopping trolley he wondered if she was one of Dr Midnight's agents too. Was there secret micro-film tucked away in the fake heel of one of her old lady shoes? Was she carrying poison mint humbugs in her handbag? Did her walking stick double up as a tranquiliser gun? Oliver would have liked to ask Agent Owl more about Dr Midnight's evil army of pensioners, but he was slumped back in his seat now, snoring loudly and drooling into his pretend beard. No wonder he was called Owl – he clearly wasn't a morning person.

When they eventually stopped, a good hour or so later, the driver opened the door and Oliver climbed out, blinking in the sunlight. He put his sunglasses back on and followed Owl to a grey warehouse with 'TOP SECRET – KEEP OUT' written across the roof in flashing red letters. There was a second, smaller sign just above the door: TOP SECRET ENTRANCE. NOTHING TO SEE HERE. Owl looked around carefully to check no one was watching, then knocked three times.

The door was opened by a man in a black suit, with a thick, curly moustache and a pink eye patch under his dark glasses.

"Ah, Oliver," he cried, shaking Oliver firmly by

the hand. "Welcome to S Service Headquarters. I'm Agent B, Head of Operation Baked Beans. I've been looking forward to working with you."

Baked beans? Oliver checked his ears for any last traces of bath water as he followed Agent B inside, wondering if he'd misheard. He found himself in a large windowless room filled with strange machines. Everywhere he looked he saw people in white coats (and dark glasses) writing things down on clipboards, but not a single bean in sight, baked or otherwise.

"Let me introduce you to some of our top-secret team," Agent B said, leading Oliver over to a funny-looking box. It turned out to be an old passport photo machine, with a woman's grinning face on the front and a short blue curtain across the doorway.

"This is Agent Fox," he said, pointing to a tall lady with ginger hair and a long nose. "She's our resident alien expert. What she doesn't know about little green men and giant two-headed purple cockroaches from the planet Xit isn't worth knowing."

Fox flashed Oliver a sharp-toothed grin.

"And this is Agent Gorilla," continued Agent B, "who heads up our jungle observation unit, and Agent Crab, our number one in underwater intelligence."

Crab – a funny-looking chap in an orange wetsuit and matching flippers – raised one of his oversized hands in greeting, before scuttling off to fetch a spanner. Oliver waved back, keeping a safe distance from Gorilla, who was so big and hairy he was bursting out of his extra-large coat.

"And finally," said Agent B, "we come to Agent Porcupine." He pointed to a round lady with spiky hair. "No one really knows what she does," he whispered, "and we're all too scared to ask her. She can be a bit prickly sometimes."

"What about that agent over there?" asked Oliver, pointing to a thin, bald man with odd socks peeking out the bottom of his trousers. "What does he do?"

"That's Norman, our S Service optician. He's in charge of dark glasses. And his wife, Neeta, is our wardrobe lady. She should be putting the finishing touches to your disguise right now in fact."

"My disguise? Like fancy dress, you mean?" Oliver was starting to like the sound of this. "Do I get to choose? I've always fancied a go as a cowboy with a lasso and a real horse... or maybe an astronaut. Have you got any spaceman suits?"

"I'm afraid not," said Agent B. "You won't be doing any space travel on this mission."

"There'll be some time travel, though," piped up Agent Fox, pointing to the photo booth. "We've just finished our final round of tests and she's all ready to go."

"Is that... is that a time machine then?" asked Oliver. "But that's impossible... isn't it?"

"Yes, it is a time machine," said Agent Fox, "and no, it's not impossible. It's actually surprisingly simple. All we've done is modify the spare time molecules you get around any kind of camera."

Huh? That wasn't *Oliver's* idea of simple.

"You know," cut in Agent Gorilla, "time molecules. They're like tiny bubbles of liquid time that slow everything down until the exact moment your smile's worn off and a pigeon's just pooed on your head... and then *snap!* That's when the camera flashes and you're caught with a grumpy frown and a sloppy white blob dripping down your forehead. Of course, in an old-fashioned passport photo booth like this one, the levels of time molecules are extra high. With only four chances to get that perfect pose, they need to be strong enough to stop time for as long as it takes for you to:

a) get bored and start redoing your hair,

b) give up and try and get your money back,

c) spin yourself round on the funny little stool until you're sick,

or d) for the next person in the queue to stick their head in and ask you if you've nearly finished.

That's when they start time running again, extra fast this time – bang, bang, bang, bang. Before you know it, you've used up all four of your photos and you're looking like a complete numpty in each one. All we have to do is harness those time molecules, run them through the trans-kinetic epoch generator and we've got ourselves a basic time machine. Like I said: simple."

"Come on," said Agent B. "Take your coat off and find a seat. I'll explain everything."

Oliver slipped off his raincoat and sat down in a black leather chair, trying not to look as puzzled as he felt. There were two more things puzzling him now:

1) What did they need a time machine for in the first place?

2) Why did his pants keep falling down under his trousers?

He had a funny feeling he'd only get the answer to *one* of those questions though.

"Now then," said Agent B. "Does the name Dr Midnight mean anything to you?"

Oliver nodded. "Agent Owl told me he's got

spies everywhere."

"That's right," said Agent B. "Dr Midnight is also one of the most clever, cunning and evil men on the planet."

"And I suppose it's your job to stop him?" Oliver guessed.

"Correction," said Agent B, "it's *our* job to stop him. And his latest plan is the cleverest, most cunning and downright evil one yet. He's been building a time machine too, only *his* model's based on a Portaloo: one of those walk-in plastic box things with a stinky toilet inside."

"I know the kind you mean. I got stuck in one on holiday last summer." Oliver shuddered at the memory. "It was *horrible*... the smelliest twenty minutes of my life... But I don't remember any time molecules flying about – how would a Portaloo time machine even work?"

Agent Porcupine swung around to face them. "Trust me," she hissed, wrinkling up her nose. "You don't want to know."

"Anyway," said Agent B, "back to Dr Midnight. We believe he's travelled to Roman Britain in his Portaloo to join forces with his great-great-great-great-more-greats-than-we've-got-time-for-great-grandfather, Gluteus Maximus, and rewrite history. Our sources tell us they're planning to make their fortune in Roman gold with nappy pins. And if there's one thing more dangerous than an evil genius, it's a rich evil genius."

"Nappy pins?" asked Oliver. They were like giant safety pins, weren't they? "What have nappy pins got to do with it?"

"Our guess is he's selling them to the Romans to help keep their togas on," said Agent B, threading an invisible nappy pin through his suit collar to demonstrate. "And that's only the beginning. He's also selling baked beans to go with their stuffed dormice, swimming trunks to wear at the baths, and popcorn to guzzle at the amphitheatre. This could change the course of history forever. That's why we need someone to stop him, Oliver. Someone who's just finished their school project on Roman Britain, who's small enough to hide in the shadows and fast enough to run away from danger. We need someone who's not scared of a few nappy pin pricks, who knows a baked bean when he tastes it, and who's willing to travel back in time for the most thrillingly dangerous assignment that's ever been assigned. We need you, Oliver Starling, with a little help from Agent Owl, to stop Dr Midnight in his fiendishly evil tracks and protect the history of our country. That," finished Agent B, "is your mission, should you choose to accept it."

"Hmmm," said Oliver. "We've got a really tricky maths test at school tomorrow. Will I be back by then?"

"Anything's possible with a time machine." Agent B winked. "But I think you might be able to miss it just this once."

"In that case the answer is 'yes'," said Oliver. "When do we start?"

CHAPTER III

It wasn't until he was changing into his tunic –
a special spy tunic with secret pockets for hiding
things in – that Oliver spotted the terrible underwear
muddle-up.

Mrs Starling must have grabbed the wrong
clothes out of the washing basket in all the royal
excitement. *Uh-oh.* She hadn't given him *his* pants
at all… which explained why they kept falling
down. But they weren't his dad's pants either.
Double uh-oh. This wasn't just a muddle-up, Oliver
realised, staring in horror at the changing room
mirror. This was a full-on underwear crisis.
A disaster!

Mum's pink frilly knickers had never looked frillier. And to make matters worse, they were her special royal ones, with glittery crowns and flowers and a picture of the Queen's head on each buttock. How was he supposed to save the world in *these*?

"Come on," called Owl through the changing room door, "they're ready for us now. The time machine's up and running."

Oliver slipped his feet into his Roman sandals, hoping for the best. So long as he kept his tunic pulled down nice and low over his knees (and his frilly knickers pulled up nice and high), no one need ever know.

"You'd better have these." Agent B handed out a mini guide to Roman Britain, which Oliver tucked into one of his secret pockets, and a purse of Roman coins for Agent Owl. Poor old Owl was squinting in the light without his beloved sunglasses on, with funny white rings around his eyes where they usually sat.

"The best of luck to both of you," added Agent

B. "Just remember, the history of our entire country – maybe even the world – depends on you."

No pressure then, thought Oliver as they squeezed into the booth.

"Ready?" asked Owl.

Oliver took a deep breath. "Ready."

"Off we go then. Say 'cheese'."

Gluteus Maximus yawned, clutching his large, gurgling belly. He'd been up late the night before with Dr Midnight, feasting on stuffed dormice and those funny little bean things from the metal container. The beans were delicious but deadly – he'd been trumping in his toga all morning. *Prrrraarrrpppp.* Gluteus let rip another shocker and belched loudly for good measure.

"Master?" A slave crept into the room, trying not to breathe in the poisonous fumes.

"Yes? What is it?" Gluteus snapped.

"The guards have found a strange object in the villa gardens, with two intruders inside."

"What sort of strange object?" Gluteus's belly gurgled louder than ever as he hauled himself onto his feet. "I suppose I'd better go and see."

He followed the slave out into the summer sunshine and waddled over to investigate. A beak-nosed man with owlish rings around his eyes stood squinting in the light, while his companion – a nervous-looking boy in a tunic – cowered behind him. Dr Midnight's black-cloaked guards already had the pair surrounded, but Gluteus was more interested in their mysterious box – a big white box with a curtained doorway and a beautiful lady's face across the front. *It must be Venus*, he decided, *the goddess of beauty and love. But what was she doing in his garden?*

"What *is* this thing?" Gluteus asked, yanking back the curtain and peering inside. "Coo-eee? Anyone home?"

"It's a photo booth," said Owl, struggling to free

himself from the muscly arms of his captor. "A special sort of machine for taking your photograph."

"Huh!" snorted Gluteus. "I'd like to see it try. No one steals *my* photograph and gets away with it. Guards! Seize this thieving booth machine at once!" He broke off for another quick burp. "What in Jupiter's name *is* a photograph, anyway?"

"Sort of like a wall painting of your face," Owl explained. "But much smaller and easier to carry around. The booth doesn't *steal* photographs though, it prints them... not that printing's been invented yet... Erm, I tell you what, why don't you try it for yourself?" He fished out a Roman sestertius from his purse. "All you have to do is sit down on the little stool, put the coin in the slot and smile at the white screen."

"This had better not be a trick," said Gluteus, eyeing him suspiciously. He turned to the biggest and burliest of the guards. "Make sure the prisoners don't try to escape," he ordered. "I've never seen such an unsavoury-looking pair." And with that he snatched up Owl's coin, climbed into the booth and pulled the curtain shut behind him.

"I'm sorry they caught us, Oliver," whispered Owl. "It was so bright without my sunglasses on, I couldn't see a thing. But don't worry, all S Service Agents are highly skilled in the art of escape. I'll think of something."

There was a flash of white light from inside the photo machine, followed by a terrible roar.

"I'm blind!" Gluteus screamed. "Holy Mercury! My eyes! My poor eyes!" There was another flash. "Aaarrrggghhhh! There it goes again! Help me, you blundering fools."

The guards all rushed at once, pushing each other out of the way in their effort to reach him. Oliver and Owl seized their chance and slipped away, slinking across the garden towards the villa. It looked just like the papier mâché model Oliver had made for his school project, only with straighter columns and less hamster droppings mixed in with the white wall paint.

Now what? Oliver wondered, as he crouched behind a sculpted marble goddess, his brain still reeling from the most amazing morning of his life. So much had happened since he climbed out of the bathtub, it was hard to take it all in. Had he really just travelled back to Roman Britain in a photo booth? Were those real-life Roman guards (with real-life sharp pointy swords) he'd just escaped from in a pair of falling-down frilly pants? And was now a good time to pull them back up, while no one was watching?

Oliver adjusted his underwear, peeping out from his statue hiding place to see Gluteus lying on the ground, clutching his eyes and shouting.

"Don't just stand there, you brainless idiots," Gluteus screamed at the unfortunate guards. "Go and find them!"

"Pssst, Owl! Have you thought of a plan yet?" Oliver asked, secretly hoping for a plan that *didn't* include angry Roman guards with sharp pointy swords.

Owl scratched his chin. "Hmm. Let's wait until the photos appear," he said, "and then make a dash for the villa toilet while Gluteus is distracted."

"The toilet? Is that where we'll find Dr Midnight's Portaloo?"

"I hadn't thought of that," Owl admitted. "To tell you the truth, I'm just rather desperate for the loo. Romans *do* have toilets, don't they?"

Oliver nodded. "We learnt all about them at school. But they don't have toilet paper… just a wet sponge on a stick."

Owl pulled a face – the exact same face Oliver's dad had pulled when Mrs Peeker's cat weed on his new work shoes. But before he could answer, there was another loud cry from the photo booth.

"It's me!" Gluteus shouted, waving around a set of passport photos. "Look, four little pictures of me! Look at that perfect bone structure, that fine Roman nose. What a handsome beast."

He was too busy admiring himself to notice Oliver and Owl creeping into the villa…

"Fast as you can now," hissed Owl as they slipped through the main entrance into the cool shade of the house.

It was even more impressive on the inside, but there was no time to stop and admire it as they darted across the central courtyard, dashing through room after room of beautiful mosaic floors without so much as a second glance. Agent Owl was a man on a mission – an urgent, sponge-on-a-stick kind of mission.

"Thank goodness," he gasped as he barrelled into the lavatory, holding his stomach.

"It's just like in the programme we watched at school," said Oliver, recognising the funny stone seats and the narrow channel cut into the floor to carry away the waste. "Well, almost…"

What he *didn't* recognise as being Roman was the blue Portaloo sitting slap bang in the middle of the room.

Owl had ignored the Roman loos and was already rattling at the door handle. "Come on, come on," he begged. "I'm not sure I can hold on much longer. Time travel does funny things to my tummy."

"*I'm* in here," came a deep voice. "You'll just have to wait."

Owl's eyes bulged. He looked nervous all of a sudden, unless that was his 'desperate for the toilet' face.

"*Grrrrrr*." The deep voice was followed by a funny growling noise. Owl looked properly scared now, unless that was his 'I *really* can't hold on any longer' face.

And then, finally, came a flushing sound. The Portaloo door swung open and a yappy little poodle in a pink knitted jacket came charging out towards the waiting agents.

"Ow!" shrieked Oliver as two sharp rows of teeth clamped tight around the back of his ankle.

"Down, Josephine," called a short, bald-headed man, stepping out of the Portaloo clutching his own personal toilet roll. His toga was edged with a broad black stripe and fastened with a large nappy pin. "No biting our guests please."

The dog released her grip on Oliver's foot with a hungry howl of disappointment. *Thank goodness!* He could feel spots of blood trickling down into his sandal.

"At least, not until we've introduced ourselves properly," added the man, locking the door behind him with a big key hanging on a chain around his neck.

"Dr Midnight!" gasped Owl. "Just as I thought." His face was positively green now.

"Agent Owl," replied the bald man, with an evil smile. "We meet again. I didn't realise my great-great-great-great-more-greats-than-we've-got-time-for-great-grandfather Gluteus had invited you. Still," he continued, the smile turning to a snarl, "it just so happens that I've converted one of the spare rooms for extra visitors who drop in unexpectedly. I like to call it the Chamber of Pain. Perhaps you and your young friend would like to see it now? I know you're going to love it."

"N-n-no thanks," stammered Oliver who was ninety-nine percent certain he *wouldn't* love the Chamber of Pain, unless it turned out to be short for the Chamber of Paintballing. "We're in a b-bit of a hurry, actually."

Owl didn't seem too keen to try it out either. He was already backing away with his legs crossed, his face looking greener than ever.

"On the count of three, start running," he whispered out the corner of his mouth. "Got it?"

"Got it," Oliver whispered back.

Dr Midnight clicked his fingers and a pair of burly guards appeared out of nowhere.

"Yes, your evilness?"

"Seize them!" shouted Dr Midnight.

"Grrrrrrrrrrrrroooooffff!" barked Josephine the poodle.

"Run!" shouted Owl. "Forget about counting to three – just run!"

Oliver ran… or at least he tried to. Time travel

seemed to have done something funny to his legs. They felt like they belonged to someone else. His falling-down pants weren't exactly helping either. Of course, they really *did* belong to someone else.

"You get the big one," he heard Dr Midnight telling the guards. "And Josephine, you get the boy." The yappy little dog set off in hot pursuit.

"Hurry, Oliver!" Owl screamed behind him. "Faster!"

Come on, Oliver told himself, *you can do this. It's just like Sports Day, only with a silly dress on and a crazy dog trying to bite off your foot.* Yes, that was better. He was really running now, running as if his life depended on it, which it probably did. Josephine the poodle had a taste for Oliver's blood and now she wanted more.

CHAPTER IV

Oliver skidded into the kitchen with Josephine right behind him. Slaves were already busy preparing the evening feast, and the air was heavy with smoke and strange cooking smells. A white-haired old lady brandished her wooden spoons at him as he tore past, muttering under her breath. Except they weren't wooden spoons at all, Oliver realised, they were knitting needles! Perhaps she was one of Dr Midnight's new Roman spies-in-training, reporting back to him on her not-so-Roman walkie-talkie: *"Enemy agent located in the kitchen. Josephine in hot pursuit. Over."*

"Oi! What do you think you're doing?" roared

the red-faced man to her left, shaking a can of baked beans at Oliver. His watery eyes bulged, his flushed forehead glistening with sweat. "You shouldn't be here."

No, thought Oliver, hurdling over a cage of fattened songbirds in his rush to get away. *I should be in Mrs Rudderson's class, practising my fractions. But I'll be the one in halves and quarters if that poodle catches me.* He dodged around a joint of meat hanging from the ceiling and lost his balance, crashing headfirst into a bowl of milk-soaked snails. *Oof! Clang! Splash!* A slippery snail shower came raining down on him like slimy confetti.

"Sorry!" he called over his shoulder, flicking the disgusting creatures off his tunic as he raced on. Josephine let out a yelp of excitement, pouncing on the swollen snails and hoovering them up like dog biscuits, her curly tail wagging with excitement as she crunched down on their shells.

That's it! thought Oliver, with a fresh burst of

hope. If he could find some more food to distract her with he might be able to get away with both his legs intact.

He grabbed at a boar's head as he ran and tucked it, still raw and bleeding, under his arm. It was too late to worry about spoiling his new tunic now, it already looked like something out of an advert for Roman washing powder: *Are you fed up with snail stains and blood all over your clothes? Then try new Brutus Urine-Rinse for whiter than white whites. Even at temperatures as low as 30 degrees and centuries before the invention of washing machines, the pure pee power of Brutus won't let you down.*

"Oi!" came an even angrier cry from behind. "What are you doing with that boar's head? Come back, thief!"

"Sorry!" Oliver called again. "Tell your master the dog stole it."

Josephine had forgotten about the snails and was right behind him now, leaping up and down and barking wildly at the smell of the meaty boar's head.

So far so good. But on the downside, two skinny looking slaves had joined in the chase as well.

"Get that head!" shouted the first one. "Or there'll be trouble!"

"Get that boy!" called the other.

Oliver swung out of the kitchen, darting back across the open courtyard towards the square rainwater pool in the centre. He took a deep breath, summoning up the last of his strength, and flung the boar's head into the middle of the pool.

Splash! It worked! There was a blur of pink jacket and white fur as Josephine leapt in after it, landing on the soggy head with a wild growl of hunger. Oliver's bitten ankle throbbed at the sight of her sharp little teeth tearing through the red flesh. That could have been him! He didn't hang around to watch though, seizing his chance to escape while the slaves were busy wading in after the dripping dog-chewed dinner. Off he raced, heading straight for the main entrance and back towards the gardens, where Gluteus was still enjoying the photo booth.

"By Juno, you're a good-looking fellow," the Roman boomed to himself from behind the curtain. "A fine figure of a man. Such smooth silky skin. Such a strong shapely jaw. Such brilliantly bushy eyebrows…"

Oliver scurried past on tiptoe, keeping to the shadows. The rest of the garden seemed suspiciously empty, apart from the little old lady knitting on a stone bench in the corner. Owl was right – Dr Midnight's spies really *were* everywhere. But where was Owl? That was the question.

Oliver slipped from tree to tree, from statue to statue, straining his eyes for a glimpse of his fellow secret agent. Hoping against hope that Owl had managed to outrun his pursuers and escape as well. But he was out of luck – and so was Owl, by the looks of it.

Now what? Oliver wondered. If he left the grounds of the villa he'd be all alone in a different time. Not so much *Agent* Starling as *Ancient* Starling. How scary would that be? And how would

Owl ever find him then? But if he stayed where he was Dr Midnight was bound to catch him. The old lady was probably reporting back to him at that very moment: *"Enemy agent spotted in the garden, pulling up his pants under his tunic. Over."* Yes, it *would* all be over if he dithered any longer. Oliver remembered the Chamber of Pain and made up his mind to get away... if he could.

"Search the gardens again for the boy!" came a low, throaty shout, as a fresh stream of guards poured out into the sunshine. "He can't have gone far."

Oliver ducked back down behind his statue, peering between the white marble legs to see guards fanning out across the grounds, sharpened swords at the ready. *Gulp!* That *definitely* decided it – he couldn't get back into the villa now, even if he wanted to. Owl would just have to manage on his own.

He turned his head, sharply, as a cart came rumbling and clattering up the road that ran alongside the gardens. Oliver remembered the old black-and-white cowboy film he'd watched when he was off school with chicken pox, where the wounded hero made his escape on the back of an old wagon. He'd never felt less like a hero than he did just then, skulking in the shadows like a cowardly runaway, but he *was* wounded, thanks to Josephine. And the old cart might be his best chance of getting out of there alive if he could reach it before the guards spotted him.

The cart was almost level with the entrance – it was now or never. Oliver's heart hammered like crazy as he eased himself up from his hiding place, steeling himself for the final dash. Was he brave enough to go through with it though? Yes… no… maybe… but then his legs answered for him, tearing out of the villa gardens at full sprint. *Keep going!* shouted his panicked brain. *Faster! Faster!*

Confused shouts followed after him on the light noon breeze.

"Look! There he is. Over there by the statue!"

"Where? I can't see him."

"No, not that statue, you brainless buffoon. That white one there."

"But they're *all* white… how am I supposed to know which one you mean?"

Oliver left them to it, pelting down the road after his rickety getaway vehicle in the fastest hundred metre race ever. Then it was straight from Sports Day sprint into the high jump, as he flung himself up, up, up towards the back of the cart.

Crash! Ow! He landed with a bump and a clatter, bashing his head against something hard and round: an empty barrel. The perfect hiding place for a runaway secret agent! Oliver clambered inside to discover a forgotten apple lurking at the bottom like a sign – a sign that it was nearly lunchtime. He was too nervous to think about eating it right now though – not with a gang of armed guards and a scary poodle still baying for his blood – so he tucked it into a tunic pocket for safekeeping and ducked down out of sight.

Oliver held his breath as the seconds ticked slowly by (or at least they would have ticked if he hadn't left his watch back at S Service headquarters, centuries in the future). *Tick. Tick. Tick.* Long seconds became long minutes and still there was no sound of the guards giving chase. No orders to stop. No hobnailed sandals clattering along the road in hot pursuit. No pointy swords poking through the wooden slats of his hiding place. Just the wild beating of his own heart, and a horrible whiff of something that had him holding his breath all over again.

When he finally dared to peep out (fresh air at last!) Oliver found himself bouncing along a dusty road, with open woodland on one side and a cemetery on the other. He'd seen Roman gravestones before, on a class trip to the local museum, but these ones looked shiny and new compared to the time-worn remains Mrs Rudderson made them copy onto their worksheets. That was the day Florence broke her glasses, Oliver remembered with a pang of homesickness. They'd flown off while she was leap-frogging over the 'Keep off the grass sign', ending up squashed under Ravi's new walking boots. There was no putting them back on after that – they were in too many pieces – and Florence had spent the rest of the trip peering into the glass cases like a cartoon mole.

Romans always buried their dead outside the town walls to avoid the spread of disease – Oliver remembered that from the museum trip too. Hopefully that's where the cart was headed now – into town. The busier the streets, the easier it would be to blend in with the locals if Dr Midnight's guards were still looking for him. But on the other hand, every single turn of the cart's wheels was taking him further away from Owl and the time machine. His relief at having escaped the Chamber of Pain gave way to a growing sense of despair. How would he get home now?

Oliver thought about his mum, waiting by the letter box in her corgi slippers and tiara for her precious invitation to the palace. There'd be no invite coming if he never made it back, would there? The best Mrs Starling could hope for then was a royal telegram explaining how he'd been lost in time. And what about his dad, hopping round the house with his weed-on work shoes, moaning about Mrs Peeker's cat and his poor throbbing toe? What if Oliver never got to hear his joke about the one-legged duck with a welly on his head again?

What if he never got to chase runaway hamsters round the kitchen on roller skates? Never got to spill half-set trifle up the dining room walls, making pretty jelly patterns all over the new curtains? Never got to practise bike jumps with Florence on the track they'd made in her grandad's field?

It wasn't only tomorrow's maths test he'd be missing if he couldn't get back to the photo booth – it was *everything*. He'd happily swap time travel for a lifetime of maths tests just to be back at school now, safe and sound, instead of lost and alone in history. If only there was someone here in Roman times he could turn to…

"Of course!" Wasn't he the great-great-great-great-more-greats-than-he-had-time-for-great-grandson of Titus Stabbicus, the famous centurion? Perhaps *he'd* be able to help. After all, they were family… sort of. And if Oliver could convince a great soldier like Titus to join forces with him against Dr Midnight, he might still have a chance. It was a long shot, but it was worth a try.

CHAPTER V

They were coming into the town now, passing under the arched gate in a slow line of carts and horses. Peeping out from his smelly barrel, Oliver saw a wide cobbled street bustling with life.

Women and slaves were heading back from the market with their shopping while sweating servants carried their masters in boxed wooden seats balanced high on their shoulders. There were people on horseback, children playing in the dirt, and a group of soldiers marching through the dust and horse poo. They didn't look like the legionaries he'd drawn in his school project though, with regular red tunics and cloaks, otherwise he might have asked *them* where to find Titus. No, their clothes were a midnight shade of black, just like the guards back at the villa. It could have only been a coincidence, but Oliver decided to play safe, ducking back down out of sight until they'd finished marching past.

As soon as the coast was clear, he hauled himself out of the barrel and jumped off the cart, in an impressive sideways roll. (He and Florence had spent all of Monday lunchtime practising their stuntman moves.) He brushed down his filthy, bloodstained tunic, hitched up his pants and tried to get his bearings, wondering where to start. What he *really* needed was a nice helpful sign marked 'Titus Stabbicus this way', or a handy tourist information office, but they hadn't been invented yet.

It was hard to think straight when everywhere was so busy. People jostled past with their fruit and vegetables, bumping at his elbows with round loaves of bread. There were noises coming at him from all directions too: a steady stream of chattering and shouting above the clatter of hooves and the rhythmic stomp of the soldiers' hobnailed sandals disappearing up the street ahead of him. And the smell? *Oh my goodness*, Oliver thought, trying not to breathe in through his nose. The smell was disgusting. It seemed to have followed him out of the barrel, mixing in with the scent of raw fish and warm dung for a pong like no other.

He chose a street at random, kicking his feet along the dusty pavement and thinking hard.

"Come on, Agent Starling, you can do this," he told himself firmly, summoning up all his skills and expertise to help him decide on a plan. There wasn't much to summon up though. The merit award he'd received for his school Roman project had been for neat handwriting and good colouring-in, not tracking down ancient relatives in a strange town. And given that colouring pencils hadn't been invented yet either, his award-winning keeping-inside-the-lines skills weren't going to be much help when it came to finding Titus.

His S Service training was no help either,

because there hadn't been any. Agent B had simply told him to keep close to Owl and do whatever he said, and Oliver had failed miserably at the first one of those already. But then, on the other hand, Owl *had* told him to run, which is exactly what Oliver had done. And now here he was, still running – running out of ideas.

He carried on down the street, hoping for a sign of some kind – for inspiration. *Let's see now... a rat chewing on a mouldy piece of bread?* No, that wasn't very inspiring. *Flies swarming round a pile of steaming horse poo?* No. That was just plain disgusting. *A stinking fish tail? A broken sandal? A dusty-looking ball of wool?* Bingo! Yes, that was a sign alright. A sign that he needed to get a move on because Dr Midnight's old lady spies could be watching him at that very moment...

Oliver picked up the abandoned wool and wiped it down on his tunic, revealing bright flamingo pink strands beneath the brown dirt. The exact same pink as Josephine's knitted coat! There was no sign of the wool's owner though, thank goodness – no brown old lady shoes sticking out of a doorway; no knitting needles clacking in the shadows or walkie-talkie whispers trailing after him. She must have dropped it earlier without realising, he decided. Or she could be on her way back for it right now.

Oliver stuffed the wool into his pocket alongside the apple and mini guide to Roman Britain (in case it came in handy for tripping up guards or flossing his teeth) and hurried over to a nearby fast food shop with a new sense of urgency.

A bored-looking man with a double chin sat slumped against the counter, twiddling his hairy thumbs and sighing to himself. It must have been lunchtime by now, but no one was buying his sausages or fried chicken. No one was buying anything.

"Excuse me?" said Oliver, his stomach rumbling at the sight of all that lovely meat. The big bowl of Secret Cereal he'd wolfed down at S Service HQ felt like a lifetime ago now.

The man looked up, his face brightening. "Yes?"

"I'm looking for Titus Stabbicus, the famous centurion."

"Oh. For a moment there I thought you might have been a customer. But I suppose you've already filled up at Burger Emperor like everyone else." The man let out another long sigh. "No one's bought anything for days – ever since that Dr Midnight fellow opened his new fast food chain. It's the beans, you see. They all want those funny baked bean things he sells. And the pies – oh yes, everyone loves his calf brain custard pies, don't they? And if they're not gorging themselves at Burger Emperor, they're stuffing their faces full of this new popcorn stuff he's selling down at the amphitheatre. Butterscotch flavour, whatever that might be. He's got them queuing right round the building for it. Can't get enough of the stuff." He sighed again. "How am I supposed to compete with that?"

"Sorry," Oliver told him. "I haven't got any money, I'm afraid. Otherwise I'd buy a couple of those chops and sausages. They smell delicious."

"Here," the man said, handing him a sausage. "Have one anyway. I'll only end up throwing them away otherwise."

"Wow! Thank you." Oliver's stomach growled in excitement. "Between you and me, I don't even like baked beans." He dropped his voice to a whisper. "They give you terrible wind."

"Tell me about it," agreed the man, breaking into a grin. "You should try sharing a bed with my wife after she's been on the bean and snail dippers. Phew. It's a wonder she doesn't blow the roof off!"

"Speaking of Dr Midnight," Oliver mumbled through a big mouthful of sausage, "I'm on a secret mission to stop him. That's why I need to find Titus Stabbicus. He's my great-great-great-great-more-greats-than-we've-got-time-for-great-grandfather."

The fast food man gave him a strange look. "He's your what?"

Oliver gulped, realising his mistake. "He's an old friend of my grandfather's," he said quickly. "But I don't know where to find him."

"He'll be up at the fort, I expect," said the fast food man, pointing over his shoulder. "It's a couple of miles out of town that way. You can't miss it."

"Thank you. And thanks again for the food. It was delicious."

The man handed him another sausage. "Go on," he said, with a wink. "Here's one for luck. Let's face it, if you're going to take on Dr Midnight, you're going to need all the luck you can get."

Oliver sat down in a doorway, cradling his second sausage, feeling a little less miserable than before. Yes, he was still centuries away from all his family and friends, but at least he had a plan now. A plan *and* a sausage. Not for long though.

"*Pssst*," came a hiss from nearby. A soft, secret kind of hiss. "Are you going to eat that or not?"

Oliver nearly dropped the sausage altogether in his excitement. "Owl?" he hissed back. "Is that you?"

"Owl? *Owl* did you say? Do I *look* like an owl to

you?"

A scowling slave girl stepped out of the shadows, bristling with indignation. A rather odd-looking slave girl, with scruffy cropped hair that was longer on one side than the other, and thick brown smears across her chin and upper lip, like a mud moustache and beard.

"If that's supposed to be a joke about my nose," she snapped, "you can stop right there."

"Huh?" Oliver hadn't even noticed her nose. It looked like a perfectly normal one to him, with the right number of nostrils and everything. A bit on the grubby side, maybe, thanks to a stray smear of mud, but other than that…

"How would you like it," she went on, "if I started making personal jokes about your sticky-out ears, or the way you smell?"

What's wrong with the way I smell? thought Oliver, stabbing himself in the eye with the sausage (ow!) as he sniffed at his armpit. *Poo-eeee.* She was right! Perhaps those whiffs in the cart hadn't been from the barrel at all. Perhaps the pong had been him all along – or his tunic, anyway. When it came to fragrances, sun-ripened snail milk and raw boar's blood was a pretty lethal combination.

"Sorry about the owl stuff," he said out loud, trying to wave the stench away with his lunch. "I didn't mean to offend you. I thought you might have been my friend."

"Your friend?" The girl cast a quick glance over her shoulder before perching down beside him. "Hmm. Friends like to share things, don't they?"

Oliver nodded, with a sudden lump in his throat. He wasn't thinking about Owl any more though. He was thinking about Florence – about everything they'd shared over the years: break-time snacks, football stickers, Trick-or-Treat sweets, jokes, secrets, twisted ankles…

"Maybe I *am* your friend after all," said the girl, eyeing up his sausage with a greedy gleam in her eye. "I'm Julia, by the way. Nice to meet you." She put out her hand and then snatched it back again, blushing furiously. "Sorry, I mean *Julius*. Silly me!"

"But I thought Julius was a boy's name," said Oliver. "Like Julius Caesar."

"Exactly," said the girl, in a much lower voice than before. "Because I *am* a boy. A man, I mean," she added, correcting herself again. "That's right. I'm a big beardy Roman citizen called Julius. You can call me Jules though, if you want. And you are?"

"Oliver," he replied, staring at her in confusion. "Oliver Starling." *A big beardy Roman citizen?* Jules looked about the same age as him – maybe even younger – and as for that beard… well, that wouldn't fool anyone. It was even worse than Owl's pirate goat effort.

Wait a minute, he thought. What if Jules was a secret agent too? Maybe her mud facial hair was a cunning disguise to avoid detection by the enemy. But who *was* the enemy? That was the question. Which side was she on?

"Well, it was lovely to meet you," he told her, hauling himself back onto his feet. A proper friend would have been nice – he'd never felt more alone in his whole life – but it was too much of a risk. If Her Majesty's S Service was recruiting children for its top-secret missions maybe Dr Midnight was doing the same, hiring slave girls to join his army of old ladies. Oliver shivered as a cloud passed over the sun. Yes, the sooner he gave Jules the slip the better.

"I must be off now though," he said. "I've got an important appointment at the er… at the…" *Don't let on where you're really going*, he told himself. *Think of something else.* But his mind had gone blank. *Dentist's? Hairdresser's? Frilly pants shop?*

"At the fort, you mean? I heard the fast food man giving you directions just now. Which is perfect," said Jules, jumping up and threading her arm through his. "Because that's where I'm going too." She grabbed hold of Oliver's sausage and took a big bite off the end. "Mmm, I love sharing, don't you? Thanks, friend."

CHAPTER VI

So much for my plan to get away, thought Oliver gloomily, as Jules dragged him through the bustling town. Trying to shake her off was like trying to shake squashed hamster poo off the bottom of a football sock: impossible. Luckily there were no signs of any black-cloaked guards chasing after them with swords. Not yet anyway.

But it was too soon to trust her, Oliver reminded himself, almost jumping out of his skin as a blur of white fur came tearing out of a doorway in front of them, barking for Britain (Roman Britain, that was). For a horrible moment, he thought it was Josephine coming to finish off what she'd started, but it turned out to be a bigger, scruffier-looking dog with a torn ear and stumpy tail – a stray, most likely.

"What's wrong?" asked Jules, sensing his panic. "You're not scared of dogs, are you?"

"No." Oliver took a deep breath, trying to control the sudden trembling in his legs. "Of course I'm not."

It was true. He wasn't scared of nice normal dogs, like Porto, Florence's farty old Labrador. Porto wouldn't hurt a fly, although he had been known to poison the odd woodlouse who strayed too near his tail end after mealtimes. No, it was only pink-coated poodles Oliver didn't like.

"I mean, it's fine if you are," said Jules, kindly. "Everyone's scared of something." She leaned in closer, her sausagey breath warm against his ear. "I'm frightened of caterpillars," she told him. "You know, those big green hairy ones with the hideous bulging eyes…" She shivered. "Just the *thought* of one gives me the creeps."

Oliver couldn't help but smile. She didn't *seem*

much like an evil spy, intent on helping Dr Midnight rewrite history and take over the world. But then, neither did Mrs Peeker, and look how wrong he'd been about her! For all he knew, this whole story about going to the fort together, as friends, was a fiendish trick – a trap. The smile died on his lips as he imagined an army of sword-wielding guards and killer poodles waiting around the next corner, ready to pounce.

No sooner had the thought of an ambush crossed his mind, than Jules swung off the main road, dragging Oliver with her. *This is it*, he thought, tensing his muscles against the coming attack as they turned onto a narrow side street, straight into the waiting arms of...

...No one. No muscly, armoured men in black, sharpening their weapons for an attack. No bloodthirsty dogs in pink, sharpening their teeth for a second helping of ankle bone chewy bites. The street was completely empty except for a stray scrap of parchment blowing along in the breeze and a skinny ginger cat, who was too busy licking his own bottom to bother with runaway secret agents.

"Are you sure this is the right way?" asked Oliver, still on high alert for a possible trap. He tugged his pants back up under his tunic, getting ready to run.

"It's a shortcut, trust me," said Jules, glancing over her shoulder for the hundredth time. Why did she keep doing that? Was she checking for hairy caterpillars or waiting for her evil genius back-up crew to arrive? Oliver glanced back over his own shoulder but there was nothing to see. Just the cat, who'd moved on from his licking to chase after the torn bit of parchment. The wind was picking up now, dancing the papery scrap along the road like a puppet, much to the cat's amusement.

"Where are you from, anyway?" asked Jules, interrupting the pantomime-style argument going on inside his head:

Watch out, it's a trap!
Oh no it isn't.

Oh yes it is. You can't trust her, she's a spy.

Oh no she isn't…

"I'm guessing you're not from round here," she said, "if you don't know which way the fort is."

Oliver didn't know what to tell her. "Me?" *I'm from a distant place called the twenty-first century. And I wish I'd never left.* "You wouldn't have heard of it. It's a long way from here. A really, really, *really* long way."

"Try me," she said. "What's it called?"

"Erm…" Even if it turned out Jules wasn't an enemy spy after all, he couldn't exactly tell her the truth, could he? *I'm from a town that doesn't exist yet. I travelled back in time in a photo booth to save the history of the world from an evil genius with a secret stash of nappy pins.* She'd never believe him. This time yesterday he wouldn't have believed it himself.

"It's called Futuria," he said at last. "Which makes me a… a Futurian."

Jules shook her head. "No, you're right, I've

never heard of it. What's it like?"

That was an easier one to answer. As long as he didn't mention cars, or phones, or computers or any of the million other things that hadn't been invented yet... Maybe not so easy after all then.

"It's great," he told her. "You'd love it. We've got bikes and skateboards and..." *No, that's no good.* "I mean comfy trainers and trousers... I mean..." He tried again. "Well, there's no such thing as slavery, for one thing. And no scary men in armour-plated dresses chasing after you with their swords. Just normal family life and school... *Everyone* has to go to school where I'm from."

Jules was drinking in his every word, her dark eyes wide with wonder. "No slavery?" she repeated. "And *everyone* goes to school? Even girls? Girls get to learn mathematics too?"

Oliver nodded. "Oh yes. My best friend's a girl and she's the best mathematician in the whole class. She's really good at football too," he added proudly, forgetting that his favourite game didn't exist yet.

"She's brilliant at everything, in fact. Except for burping. I can do *much* better burps than her."

He was about to offer Jules a demonstration when he spotted a tear in the corner of her eye.

"It sounds amazing," she said with a loud sniff. "You're so lucky. But who knows. Maybe I'll get to see it for myself one day. That's why I'm joining the army," she told him, forcing her mouth back into a smile. "To see the world."

"Joining the army?" Oliver repeated, trying not to laugh. "You?"

At least that explained the bonkers brown beard and false name: only men were allowed to serve as soldiers. It wasn't a spy disguise after all then.

"But you're…" He broke off, not wanting to hurt her feelings. Now he knew Jules wasn't an enemy agent, maybe they really *could* be friends after all. She reminded him of Florence in some ways. She had the same determined gleam in her eye, the same mischievous grin. Not that she was grinning any more, though – quite the opposite.

"I'm what?" asked Jules, sticking out her chin and glaring at him. "What were you going to say?"

"You're… you're… not tall enough," finished Oliver. Didn't you have to be a certain height to become a legionary? Jules was no bigger than he was.

She pulled herself up onto her tiptoes, spitting on her hand and ruffling her short hair so that it stood up on end. "I'm perfectly tall, thank you very much. Of course they'll let me in. They *have* to, otherwise…" She sniffed again. "I can't go back," she said quietly. "I'll be in so much trouble. I'm not really a Roman citizen at all. I'm a slave. And you know what they do to runaways, don't you?"

They probably didn't give out many 'Congratulations on your Successful Escape' certificates, Oliver knew that much. The Romans could be pretty ruthless when it came to handing out punishments, like executing one in every ten soldiers to teach rebellious army units a lesson. And some punishments were just too gruesome to think about… imagine being torn apart by lions in an amphitheatre. What a horrible way to go!

"You're on the run too?" he said, changing the subject to try and take her mind off it. "Snap!" Oliver was the one glancing over his shoulder now, dropping his voice to a low whisper. "Have you heard of Dr Midnight? The world's number one evil genius?"

"I've heard of *a* Dr Midnight," said Jules. "The world's number one nappy pin and baked bean salesman." She thought for a moment. "In fact, he's probably the world's number one Burger Emperor builder too. There seem to be more branches popping up every day. Is that who you mean?"

Oliver nodded. "There's more to him than pins and pies though. He's already caught my friend Owl and now he's after me. I need to keep out of his Chamber of Pain or I'll *never* get home again. In fact, even if he *doesn't* lock me up and throw away the key, I don't know how I'm going to get back to my family now. Everything's gone wrong," he told her, picturing poor old Owl locked up in Dr Midnight's famous chamber. For some reason, Oliver imagined a nail-studded cell, with red molten lava swishing across the floor and an army of guards playing Hot Cross Buns on the recorder through a tiny slit in the door. He shuddered at the thought. That really *would* be painful.

"I must be the worst secret agent in the history of secret agents," he said, wishing he'd never accepted the mission in the first place. "That's why I need to find Titus Stabbicus, the famous centurion. I can't do this on my own."

"I don't know what a secret agent is, I'm afraid," said Jules, squeezing his hand. "But what I *do* know is you're not on your own. You've got me now. It's going to be alright. You'll see. We'll find this Titus together and ask him to save your friend. And who knows, maybe he'll find me a place in his century too."

His century?

"What do you mean?" asked Oliver, a fresh

bubble of hope swelling inside his chest, but Jules seemed to have drifted off into her own dream-world. Maybe she was some kind of time-traveller too, he thought. Maybe he could borrow *her* time machine to get back home. Yes! Then he could fetch Agent Gorilla to rescue Owl and save the day. Gorilla was twice the size of Dr Midnight's guards – they'd be too scared to use their swords on him.

It was the perfect plan. Or at least it would have been, until he remembered that 'century' was the name for a unit of Roman legionaries. Jules wasn't a time-traveller at all, was she? Just a runaway slave girl with funny-looking hair and an even funnier-looking beard. Oliver's bubble of hope burst like an over-blown balloon.

He sank back into silence, the gathering grey clouds above his head matching his gloomy mood. For a moment there he thought he'd found a way out – a way back home. But no, here he was, stuck in the past whether he liked it or not.

And if his great-great-great-great-more-greats-than-we've-got-time-for-great-grandfather Titus couldn't help him, he didn't know *what* he'd do.

CHAPTER VII

"Woah," said Jules, as they finally left the town walls behind them, heading up the hill towards the fort. "What's going on here?"

It was a good question. The once straight Roman road wasn't looking quite so straight anymore, thanks to the brand new bend being built in the middle. One team of slaves was hard at work levering up the top paving stones from the old route, while another group hacked out a fresh trench for the replacement section, curving away towards a low building on the horizon.

"Has the fort moved, or something?" asked Jules, squinting into the distance. "Is that why you're changing the roads round?"

One of the soldiers in charge (a proper-looking one this time, with a red cloak and tunic) chuckled to himself.

"No, no, no. Nothing to do with the fort," he said, patting his rounded stomach. "It's that new ride-through Burger Emperor they've opened up. Best snail dippers for miles around, and you don't even have to climb off your horse to get them. There's a special offer on this week, too. Buy a hundred get one free! But it's no good opening up a ride-through restaurant if no one can get to it."

Oliver groaned. *Dr Midnight strikes again!* It would take the army twice as long to march anywhere if they kept putting bends in all the roads. That's if the soldiers had any energy left for marching after eating all that extra food. And if Dr Midnight kept messing around with the past, what would that do to the future? To *his* future?

"Oh dear. Tummy ache?" asked the soldier cheerily, mistaking Oliver's groans of despair for trapped wind. "I know the feeling. That last calf brain custard pie was a big mistake after all my dippers, but it looked so tasty… Almost as tasty as the date and popping candy one I had in town yesterday. It's that Dr Midnight," he said, laughing again. "His pies are everywhere!"

"His *spies* are everywhere too," said Oliver, his despair deepening as a grey-haired old lady came tottering along the road behind them, pushing a foldaway shopping trolley. It was probably filled with balls of wool and a walkie-talkie, ready to update Dr Midnight: *"Enemy agent spotted on road to new Burger Emperor. Current pants status unconfirmed. Target now travelling in company of slave girl with normal nose and strange beard. Over."*

"Here's one of Dr Midnight's spies now," Oliver whispered to Jules, pointing down the hill towards the slowly-advancing pensioner.

"Trust me," he said, seeing the look of amused disbelief on his friend's face. "She's more dangerous than you'd think – one word from her and we'll have a whole army of guards chasing after us. I bet she's a secret knitting needle ninja too."

"A secret what?" asked Jules, wrinkling up her nose in confusion. Funnily enough it *did* look a bit like an owl's beak when she did that.

"Er… sort of like a gladiator," he explained, "only with thin, spiky sticks instead of swords."

He thought for a moment. "Perhaps we should try and find another way to the fort instead – one with more hiding places. We might be able to outrun Knitting Nora there, but Dr Midnight's guards are a different matter. Unless you'd rather split up?" he said. "It's me they're after, not you."

Jules shook her head. "I told you, we're a team now… and you did share your sausage with me."

You didn't exactly give me much choice, thought Oliver, chuckling inwardly at the memory.

"Besides," added Jules, "this Titus of yours could be my best chance of joining the army, and they'll never let me in to see him on my own. Either we track him down together, or not at all."

I'll go for the first option, thought Oliver, crossing his fingers for luck. *Please let it be the first one.* He looked around for an alternative route to the fort – through those dark, scary-looking woods over there, perhaps?

"Come on, hurry up you lot," the round-bellied soldier told his sweating workers. "The sooner we get this new road finished, the sooner I can try out my new swimming trunks in the bath house. I *was* going to wear them for sunbathing, but it looks like there's a storm coming in." He sighed a long homesick sigh. "Thirteen years I've been stationed here in Britain," he said, turning back to Oliver and Jules, "and the weather never gets any better. The damp air does rotten things to a fellow's feet too. You should have seen the state of them when I took my sandals off last night. In fact, you can see them now if you want?"

"It's tempting," lied Oliver, "but we really need to be going. There is something you can do for us though. You see that sweet little old lady coming up the hill? If she asks which way we went, tell her…" He racked his brains for a suitable story to throw Dr Midnight off the scent. "Hmm. Tell her we're heading to the new ride-through to pick up some snail dippers," he said at last.

"But you haven't got a horse," pointed out the soldier. "You'd be better off at the new march-through Burger Emperor they're building further up the road."

"No, that's okay," said Oliver. "I don't even like snails. If you could just tell her that anyway. Thank you," he added, as he and Jules set off towards the spooky-looking woods.

It was dark and gloomy under the heavy canopy of trees. Maybe the soldier was right – maybe there was a storm coming. It was a pity Dr Midnight hadn't introduced the Romans to the delights of raincoats yet – a waterproof coat might have come in handy.

Birds cackled and cawed above their heads as

Oliver and Jules clambered and slipped over fallen logs. Sharp brambles scratched at their bare legs. If there *was* a proper path through the trees, they must have missed it. Little biting flies batted at their faces while small woodland creatures followed along behind, rustling and snuffling through the undergrowth. At least Oliver hoped that's what they were. Not sniffly spies with blocked-up noses. Or big wild boars with sharp tusks. Or a pack of hungry wolves tracking their scent…

"Which way now?" Oliver asked, once Jules had sucked the last bit of juice out of their shared apple.

A fat drop of rain splashed on the end of his nose, as if to remind him that their break was over. He didn't feel very rested though. Agent B had warned him the mission might be dangerous, but he hadn't mentioned how tiring it would be. All that running around and escaping had taken its toll on Oliver's weary muscles and blistered feet. His brain was exhausted too. A tricky maths test was nothing compared to trying to puzzle his way through Roman Britain without getting caught.

He twisted round on the spot, trying to get his bearings. "The old road's somewhere over there, isn't it? Or is it back that way? I've lost all sense of direction."

"This way," said Jules confidently, wiping rain out of her eyes with one hand and pointing through the trees with the other.

Phew! Oliver breathed a secret sigh of relief. At least one of them knew where they were going. For a second or two, he thought they were lost.

"Or do I mean this way?" said Jules. "No. That's where we've just come from. Isn't it? Or did we come from down there?"

It all looked the same – that was the problem. Trees, trees and more trees. For all Oliver knew, they'd been going around in circles this whole time.

"Perhaps coming through the woods was a stupid

idea," he said. "Sorry Jules. You'd probably have been there by now if it wasn't for me."

"No I wouldn't. I'd still be hiding away by that fast food shop, too scared to come out of the shadows in case my master spotted me. I thought I'd *done* the tricky bit – the actual escaping – but it turns out *staying* escaped is even trickier. I'll let you into a little secret," she added, dropping her voice, as if the trees themselves might be listening in. "You know when I told you I'm not really a Roman citizen?"

Oliver nodded.

"Well I'm not really a big, beardy man either. I painted this on myself as a disguise."

She rubbed at the side of her chin to demonstrate. The caked-on mud had grown soft and slimy in the rain, smudging up her cheek in a big ugly smear.

"Gosh!" said Oliver, trying to look surprised. "I'd never have guessed."

"Really?" Jules seemed pleased. "I wasn't sure if it would fool anyone or not. I was going to try it out on the fast food man, only I hadn't quite plucked up the courage yet. That's what I was doing when you found me."

"Well I'm glad I did. I'm glad we found each other." Even in the cold and wet, Oliver felt a warm glow inside. They really must be friends now if Jules trusted him enough to tell the truth. But the warm glow quickly gave way to a sharp twinge of guilt as he remembered all the secrets he was keeping from her.

"It's time I was honest with you too," he said. "You probably won't believe me, and that's fine – I can hardly believe it myself – but you deserve to know who I really am... Where I'm really from..."

He took a deep breath, trying to think of the best place to start. *I was in the bath this morning, washing trifle out of my hair...* No. That was no good. Romans didn't have trifle, did they? Maybe he should skip that bit. And the bit about the royal wedding bunting and the big bar of chocolate. They might be tricky too. And the bit about the car...

Hmm. Perhaps he was going about this all wrong.

"Remember when I told you I was from a place called Futuria?" he said at last.

Jules nodded.

"Well I lied. I'm from a little town called Gobbleford. And you *definitely* won't have heard of it because it hasn't been built yet. I expect it's all still woods right now – just like this – or boggy marshland. Or one big dreary nothing as far as the eye can see."

Jules looked confused again. "How can it be nothing? There must be *one* house there at least. Yours, I mean. You must live *somewhere*."

"Oh yes," said Oliver. "I live in a lovely house, with hot and cold running water, central heating, nice warm beds and a big fridge full of tasty food. And when I say 'tasty food' I don't mean snails. All our snails live out in the garden with the slugs."

It was funny really, he thought, as another wave of homesickness washed over him. He'd never realised quite how lucky he was until today.

"I live with my mum and my dad and my hamster, Mr Puffy-Cheeks," he went on. "Come to think of it, Mr Puffy-Cheeks is a bit of a runaway too. A runaway champion in fact. The moment you open his cage to give him some food, *whoosh*, he's off again, nibbling at homework, tripping Mum up with her trifle, pooing all over the kitchen floor... Only that's the problem. There's no kitchen floor to be pooed on yet. No Mum, no Dad, no anything. All that belongs in the future. And so do I. If it wasn't for my merit-awarded history project and the photo booth, plus something to do with time molecules that's too complicated for anyone to understand, I'd still be there now. *That's* why I need Titus Stabbicus to help me," he finally finished. "I have to get that photo booth back and rescue Owl. And after *that* there's just the small matter of defeating Dr Midnight and saving the history of the world as we know it."

It was no good. Jules had given up looking confused now. She just looked blank. It was the same blank expression Mr Starling wore on holidays to France whenever anyone spoke to him in French.

"I belong in a different century," said Oliver, trying again.

"A century?" *That* got her attention, but not for the right reason. "Why didn't you tell me you were a soldier? Is that how you know Titus Stabbicus? Ooo, this is perfect," she said, flinging her arms around his shoulders. "You'll be able to give me all your soldiery tips on the way there... Ugh," she added, pulling away again. "That tunic of yours doesn't get any less smelly, does it?"

Oliver's cheeks flushed with heat. He wasn't sure if it was the hug making him blush, or embarrassment over his odour issues, but Jules didn't seem to have noticed. She was still chattering away about his tunic:

"It doesn't look too good either with all that blood down the front and that big patch of mud on your bottom where you tripped over that root. I just hope the fort guards let you in when we finally get there. I don't know what soldiers are like back in Gobblefrog but they're pretty neat and orderly round here…"

"It's Gobble*ford*," said Oliver. "Not *frog*. And I'm not a soldier, I'm a schoolboy."

Jules was right about one thing though, he realised, glancing down at his filthy outfit. He looked a mess. What would Titus Stabbicus think when his great-great-great-great-more-greats-than-we've-got-time-for-great-grandson turned up looking like he'd escaped from a bad washing powder advert? *Is your so-called distant relative a filthy, smelly embarrassment to the family name? Don't bother trying new Brutus Urine-Rinse. Have him publicly whipped for his cheek instead and send him on his way.* "I *could* do with a bit of a clean-up before we get there," he admitted, licking his finger and rubbing at a stray splatter of boar's blood.

"In that case, we'll go this way," said Jules. "I think I can hear water – a river or something. That ought to do the trick. And once you're cleaned up we might as well follow it. I can't promise it will lead us to the fort but it's bound to lead somewhere."

CHAPTER VIII

Jules was right – it was a river. A fast, churning river chasing along the mini cliff at the edge of the woods in a foaming torrent of white. And there in the distance, on the other side of the water, stood the fort. Things couldn't have worked out any better! It was just like the one Oliver had drawn for his school project too, with battlements and watchtowers along the outer walls and an impressive arched gateway cut into each side: North, South, East and West. From his high viewing point on the rocks Oliver could pick out all the different buildings inside, from the fort commander's house next to the headquarters, to the granary stores and the barracks, where the soldiers slept.

"We did it!" he said, turning back to Jules with a grin of triumph. "*You* did it, I mean. It was your idea to try and find the river. Best plan ever! I wonder which block Titus's rooms are in?" He leaned out over the rock for a better view. "Centurions get their own special quarters, don't they? Although he might still be out on patrol somewhere at the moment..."

The rain was lashing down on them like sharpened arrows now, but Oliver was too excited to care. It seemed like his luck was finally starting to change.

"I don't even know what he looks like," he realised. "I guess if he's from Dad's side of the family he'll be tall and skinny, with a bald patch and a love of terrible jokes. And if he's from Mum's side he'll be shorter, with frizzy orange hair and corgi slippers. Okay, maybe not the slippers... Wait a minute, perhaps there's a picture of him in the book Agent B gave me."

Oliver had forgotten all about his mini guide to

Roman Britain until now, but it was still there, tucked away in the secret pocket of his tunic with the pink ball of wool he'd found in the street. It was a little soggier than before, thanks to the cold wet seeping through his clothes, but Oliver was able to peel the pages apart without too much trouble. They didn't make for very good reading though. His heart sank as he flicked from one section to another. He was too late – the history of Roman Britain had already changed. It was all right there in the book.

There was a whole page about the bendy Roman roads, taking people from one branch of Burger Emperor to another, and a special section on the army's junk food diet. Soldiers had grown lazy, too, according to the book, sunbathing along Hadrian's Wall in their swimming trunks when they should have been out marching and training and building things.

It looked like the changes to Roman life Oliver had spotted today were only the beginning though, in this new version of history. As the regular army grew weaker, Dr Midnight's private band of slave soldiers grew stronger and stronger until... *Oh my goodness*. There was a picture of Dr Midnight on the very last page, only he wasn't called *Dr* Midnight anymore. He was *Emperor* Midnight. Oliver snapped the book shut again, shuddering at the very thought.

"Did you find a picture of him?" asked Jules, as he tucked the book back into his pocket.

Oliver shook his head, still too shocked to speak. *Emperor Midnight*? No wonder Her Majesty's S Service wanted him stopped.

"Oh well, never mind," she said. "I'm sure someone will know where to find him. Besides, we've got bigger problems right now than tracking down your centurion."

"What?" Oliver spun round, expecting to see black-cloaked guards in hot pursuit. Or an army of needle-wielding old ladies, all whispering into their walkie-talkies at once: *Enemy agent located by river on edge of woods. Current status of companion's beard: high level of smudge with increased dripping. Over.* But there was no one there. Just the thick gloom of trees and an evil-looking patch of stinging nettles.

"What do you mean?" he asked, hoisting his underwear back up while Jules was busy looking the other way. The rain had gone into the frilly bits making them droopier than ever.

"I mean how are we going to get across *that*?" said Jules, pointing to the rushing water below. "I was thinking of a nice gentle little river for you to wash your clothes in, not a big crashing monster like that. It's no good finding the fort if we can't actually get there."

Oliver hadn't thought of that. Maybe it *wasn't* the best plan ever after all. No, the best plan ever would have included a bridge over to the other side, with a handy stall on the far bank giving out free tunics and underwear for all. Maybe even a free time machine while they were at it, and a copy of *The Idiot's Guide to Tackling Evil Geniuses and Saving the World.*

"What about those stepping stones over there?" he said, pointing upstream. "If we can find a safe way down to the water we might be able to get across that way."

Jules didn't look convinced. "It sounds a bit dangerous to me."

Yes, it probably was. But then everything Oliver had done since he first set foot in the photo booth that morning had been dangerous, apart from eating his lunch. It was a pity he couldn't use his sausage-munching skills to defeat Dr Midnight instead – a hot dog-eating contest would have been a much more civilised way to go about things. First one to a hundred wins. On your marks... get ketchup... go!

"It'll be fine," he said, sounding more confident than he felt. "Look, there's a bit of a path down this way. Follow me."

It was hard-going without proper walking boots and a hood. The rocks were wet and slippery and the weather made it difficult to see where they were putting their feet. But the thought of Emperor

Midnight taking over the empire for his own evil ends drove Oliver on through the biting rain. It wasn't just Owl who needed rescuing anymore – it was the whole of history.

"Now what?" asked Jules.

What little path there was had run out altogether halfway down the mini cliff, leaving them stranded above a sheer drop.

"It's too far to jump – we'll never make it down in one piece. I knew this was a bad idea." She looked cold and miserable, with mud dripping off the end of her chin and her once-spiky hair plastered flat against her scalp.

Oliver looked around for inspiration, determined not to give up now – not when they were so close. There wasn't much to look at though, apart from slimy rocks, wet moss, and the broken old stump of a tree. But that was enough, as it turned out – enough for the greatest getting-down-from-a-mini-cliff idea in the entire history of mini-cliff ideas.

"Don't worry," he told Jules. "We don't need to

jump. I've got a much better plan."

He tested the broken tree trunk to check if it would take his weight – so far so good – and then reached back into his tunic pocket for the pink ball of wool he'd found earlier. "I *knew* this would come in useful. How's your finger knitting?"

"My what?"

"Finger knitting. Florence taught me how to do it last summer," Oliver explained, remembering the long stripy snake they'd knitted out of his mum's leftover wool. It was still at the bottom of his wardrobe waiting to be made into a hamster lasso.

"Don't worry," he told her. "It's pretty easy once you get the hang of it."

"But I thought knitting was what evil spies do? Like that Knitty Nora you spotted following us up the road?"

"True," Oliver admitted. "It's not just for baddies though. My mum knitted herself a pair of corgi slippers and *she's* not evil… apart from when she says I can't play on the computer because I have to do my homework. But that doesn't really count."

"So now you're going to be a Knitty Nora too?" asked Jules, her nose set to full-on wrinkle.

"Yes," said Oliver. "And you can be my assistant. We'll be Noras together. And once we've knitted our rope we can hook it over the tree stump and lower ourselves down to the river."

"Oh, I see! That's a good idea. Come on then, show me what to do."

It took Oliver a few goes (and rather a lot of knots) to remember which threads went where. His assistant turned out to be a natural though, so they swapped over, with Jules in charge of the knitting bit and Oliver in charge of tangles and telling cheery jokes to take their mind off the weather.

"What do you call a one-legged duck with a welly on his head?"

But even with Jules's nimble fingers on the job it was still a slow, painful process and the jokes ran out long before the wool did.

"There," she said finally, holding up the skinny

woollen snake. The wet wool had rubbed her hands raw and her teeth were chattering with the cold. "All finished."

"Brilliant," said Oliver, flashing her an encouraging smile. And it was brilliant, too – what there was of it. He'd been imagining something a bit longer – long enough to get them all the way down to the river below. But it would just have to do.

"I'll go first, if you want," he offered, triple-knotting one end of the snake around the tree stump. It *seemed* strong enough. "There's still going to be a bit of a jump at the bottom, I'm afraid."

Jules re-examined the rocky drop below them, shivering like mad. "No, I'd rather get it over and done with. Besides, I'm lighter than you," she joked. "You might snap the wool and leave me stranded!"

The time for jokes had passed though – neither of them were laughing now. Jules tugged down on the pink snake, testing the knots for herself. "You're sure it's safe?"

"Of course," said Oliver, crossing his fingers

behind his back. *Please, please let it be safe.* "But maybe I *should* go first after all," he added. "Just in case. I'd hate for anything to happen to you."

Jules was having none of it. "I'm going to be a soldier, remember. How will I be brave enough for battle if I can't manage a wet woolly Nora snake?" And with that she grabbed hold of the pink rope and swung herself out onto the cliff face, like a mountaineer. "Wish me luck!"

Oliver wanted to shut his eyes until it was all over, but that wouldn't help Jules. He forced himself to watch instead, holding his breath as she inched herself down the rope, one shaking handhold at a time. The fibres in the wool stretched and strained under her weight, the old tree-trunk creaking in sympathy. But everything seemed to be holding. Yes! It was working. It was actually working! Maybe it was going to be okay. Maybe he wasn't such a terrible secret agent after all.

"Watch out Dr Midnight," he muttered under his breath. "Here we c–"

The word died on his lips as a sudden rumble of thunder shook the air. Jules twisted round in shock, kicking out at the rock with her sandals as the wet wool slipped through her fingers and she toppled backwards in slow motion.

For a moment she looked as if she was swimming, her arms paddling wildly through the empty air as her mouth opened in a wide O of terror. And then...

And then nothing.

She was gone.

CHAPTER IX

What had he done? Why had he told her it was safe? Oliver was too stunned to move at first. Too scared to look. But then, as the rolling thunder died away, he heard a faint *help* from below.

"Jules?" He grabbed hold of the tree stump and leaned out over the cliff. "Is that you?"

A pale shape lay still against the dark mud of the river bank.

"Jules?" he called again. Why wasn't she moving? Was she hurt?

"Of course it's me!" came her rather less faint reply. "Don't just stand there gawping like a snail brain. HELP!"

"Hold on, I'm coming down," he called, grabbing hold of the abandoned wool-rope and swinging out onto the rock face. The wind must have carried her answer away. The only sound from below was the wild rush of the river roaring through the valley. But Oliver kept on talking to her just the same. Or maybe it was himself he was really talking to.

"Stay calm. That's it. No need to panic now. Everything's going to be okay."

Climbing down a homemade rope in the middle of a storm was harder than it looked. Much harder. But he forced himself on, wet wool chafing at his hands and thighs as he wriggled and slithered his way down. *Please don't break*, he begged the straining wool beneath his fingers. *Please don't let me fall.* He'd be no good to anyone, especially Jules, if he broke his leg now. Or worse…

He was so busy trying not to slip, he didn't notice how far he'd come. It wasn't until his fingers closed round empty air that he realised the rope had run out.

And it must have stretched further than he thought because the ground was within jumping distance now. It would take a big jump – a *really* big jump – but he shut his eyes, imagining a soft, squidgy pile of gym mats waiting underneath, and leapt.

"Geronimo!"

Crash!

"Ow!"

He landed on a hard, un-squidgy pile of stones, with something that felt suspiciously like a thistle digging in through his frilly knickers. But apart from a new rip along the bottom of his tunic, everything seemed to be in one piece. Nothing broken. And there, watching the whole episode through pain-filled eyes, lay Jules, her left ankle swelling up like a cartoon puffer fish.

"Are you alright?" Oliver asked, although he could see from the state of her foot that she wasn't.

Jules nodded bravely as he knelt down beside her. "I will be. I just need you to help me up." She dragged herself onto her bottom. "I need you to…

ow, ow, ow, OW!"

"No, don't try and stand on it," Oliver said, trying to remember what the doctors had said when his favourite footballer sprained his ankle. Something to do with rice, wasn't it? All he could think of was the rice in his mum's chicken risotto, all delicious and creamy and covered in melted cheese, but that wasn't much help. No, wait, it wasn't rice at all – he remembered looking it up on his dad's laptop – it was R.I.C.E. Which stood for Rest, Ice, something beginning with 'C' that meant wearing a special sock to keep the swelling down, and Elevation. Yes, that was it. Unfortunately he didn't haven't any ice or special socks, just cold rain and blister-rubbing sandals.

"You're going to have to stay there and rest, I'm afraid," he told Jules. "With your foot up in the air. There's nothing else for it. I'll ask Titus to send a stretcher for you when I get there."

"I can't stay here," she said, looking horrified. "There might be caterpillars! Are you going to help me or not?"

"Okay," he agreed, easing her up onto her good foot and guiding her across to a nearby rock. "I might not have any socks but I *do* have a ripped tunic," he added, as another brilliant idea flashed into his brain, like the lightning bolt above his head. Dr Midnight wasn't the only genius round here!

Oliver grabbed hold of the loose flap of material along the bottom hem and pulled, tearing off a long thin strip like a bandage.

"Now sit still while I make you a sock-thing for your ankle," he said. "And then…" *Pow! Another genius idea!* They were coming thick and fast now. "And then I'll get you some sticks to use as crutches."

Oliver's ideas might have been brilliant but his first aid skills weren't. It took him seventeen attempts (and a lot of wincing from Jules) to get the bandage right but the crutches proved much easier. The storm had brought down two sturdy branches a little way further down the river, with handy Vshaped off-shoots at one end for Jules to tuck under her armpits.

"They're a bit scratchy," she said, limping slowly along the riverbank. "But I think they'll do the trick. You might have to give me a lift across the stepping stones though."

Oliver had been thinking the same thing. He'd also been thinking about roast chicken for some reason. Perhaps it was the wishbone-shaped tops of Jules's crutches, or the roast potato shapes of the stepping stones themselves, rearing up out of a churning brown river of gravy… *No!* He forced all homesick thoughts of dinner back out of his head, flinging the crutches over to the far bank like javelins, before hoisting Jules up onto his back. She lurched sideways as he caught her ankle with her elbow, crying out with pain.

"Sorry!" Oliver struggled to regain his balance. "You'll have to sit stiller than that," he told her. "If you fall off in the river, I'll never catch you."

And if I fall off we're both done for. He was okay

at swimming in a nice warm pool, with the shallow end only a few strokes away and a friendly lifeguard watching on. But the river was a different matter. They'd be swept away before they knew what was happening, dashed against the rocks like a pair of rag dolls.

He took a deep breath, steeling himself for the task ahead. The first few stepping stones looked easy enough but the ones in the middle of the river were much more spaced out. He wasn't even sure his legs would stretch that far. *Don't think about that now*, he told himself. *Think what you're going to say to Titus when you finally get there.*

Excuse me, Mr Stabbicus, sir. Was that the right way to address a centurion? Oliver's school project hadn't covered things like that. *You don't know me but I'm a distant relative of yours from er... from Futuria. And I really need your help. Dr Midnight's kidnapped my friend and now he's taking over the whole country with his baked beans and swimming trunks and trying to make himself Emperor. I was wondering if you and your soldiers could come and catch him for me? And his dog, of course. We mustn't forget Josephine...*

That was where Oliver's distraction tactics ran out though. They'd reached the middle of the river already. Jules seemed to have doubled in weight and the next stepping stone looked a scarily long way away.

"You can do this," came a soft whisper in his right ear. "After three now: one... two... three."

Oliver didn't move. He *couldn't* move. His feet seemed to have glued themselves to the stone.

"I can't," he said. "It's too dangerous."

Jules tried again. "You escaped from Dr Midnight, didn't you? And you climbed down a cliff on a tiny little Nora rope in the middle of a storm. You even made me a sock out of your tunic, without caring that people can see the frilly pink bits on your underwear now. There's *nothing* you can't do, Agent Starling."

Oliver nodded solemnly, pulling up his pants and

readying himself for the jump. Jules was right. *Oliver* Starling might be too scared to take the next step, but *Agent* Starling wasn't.

"For Queen and Country!" he cried, leaping across the gap like a gazelle – a gazelle with a rhino strapped to its back. He didn't even stop to adjust his footing once he got there, leaping straight on to the next stone and the one after that, bounding all the way over to the other bank before he could change his mind.

"You did it!" cried Jules, giggling with relief. "I know I *said* you could, but I didn't think you'd manage it so easily. Oh, thank goodness for that!"

Yes, thought Oliver, giddy with the delayed shock of what he'd just done. *Thank goodness*. Now all he had to do was find Titus, convince him to abandon his duties to help a scruffy-looking relative he'd never heard of, save Owl from the Chamber of Pain, and put an end to Dr Midnight's dastardly plans once and for all. Easy!

CHAPTER X

The closer they got to the fort, the more impressive it looked, with its high stone walls and deep defensive ditch running all the way around the outside. There was plenty of time to admire it during their long, limping approach. The storm had finally moved on, but even without the rain battering at their faces, progress was still painfully slow.

"Oo… ow… oo… ow," said Jules, grimacing with every step. "Maybe you *should* go on ahead without me after all, caterpillars or no caterpillars. It'll be dark by the time we get there otherwise. What if they've shut the gates for the night?"

"Then we'll just have to wait until morning,"

said Oliver, too exhausted by the day's events to go much faster himself. "We're a team, remember. We find Titus together or not at all."

"I'm not sure there's any point," she said. "For me, I mean. I was stupid to think I could ever be a soldier. Look at me. I'm just a skinny little slave girl with badly cut hair and a sprained ankle."

"That's not what *I* see when I look at you," Oliver told her. "I see someone brave and fearless who'll try anything to make her life better. And yes, you're right," he admitted. "They probably *won't* let you in the army, but once we've defeated Dr Midnight and got the photo booth back, you can come and live with me instead. In the future."

He wasn't sure what Mrs Starling would think of that – it had taken her long enough to agree to a hamster, let alone a runaway Roman slave – but he'd worry about that when the time came. All he knew was he couldn't leave Jules here on her own. Not with a bad ankle and no roof above her head. Without so much as a sausage to her name.

"Really?" she said. "Back to Gobblefrog, you mean?" She seemed to have forgotten about the pain in her ankle now. Her eyes were shining with excitement. "To your school for girls?"

Oliver nodded. "Girls *and* boys. Everyone gets to go to school in the future, whether they like it or not."

He was going to warn her about homework, and maths tests, and the watery cabbage they served every Wednesday lunchtime, but he never got the chance. He was interrupted by a loud clatter of horse hooves coming along the road behind them, and a low booming voice calling for them to stop. It was a soldier – a tall, important-looking one with a big feathered plume in his helmet.

"Woah!" said the soldier, circling his horse round in front of them and pulling it to a halt. "What are you two doing out here so close to sundown?"

"We've come to see Titus," Oliver told him, pulling himself up straighter and smoothing down his wet tunic. This was it. The success of his whole mission depended on what happened next. "Titus Stabbicus," he added, just to be clear.

The soldier laughed. "Titus Stabbicus, eh? I don't think so, young man."

"Please, sir," said Oliver. "It's important. A matter of life and death." No one was dying yet, admittedly, but that was only a matter of time. "You *have* to let us see him or… or…" Or what?

"Listen, we've come all this way to talk to him," said Jules, fixing the soldier with a determined stare. "And we're not leaving until we do."

The soldier laughed again. "You'll have a long wait then, won't you? Titus retired from the army last week. I couldn't tell you where he is now, I'm afraid, although I hear he's doing very well for himself. Invested in a job lot of Dr Midnight's nappy pins and set himself up making birthday badges."

"Birthday badges?" Jules repeated. "What do you mean?"

"You know, different badges for different ages. 'I am VI' or 'XVIII today' – that kind of thing.

They've been selling like crazy. Hooray for Dr Midnight, that's what I say. Hey, have you tried those baked beans of his? Deeeeeelicious."

"He can't have retired," said Oliver. "He just can't."

How was he going to save Owl now?

The soldier nodded. "I'm afraid so. It looks like you've had a wasted journey, doesn't it?"

"And he's gone into business with Dr Midnight?" Oliver was still struggling to take it all in. "You're saying they're on the same side now?"

"I'm *saying* he's set himself up making birthday badges. How many times do I have to tell you?"

"But… but…" Oliver didn't know what to say. He didn't even know what to think anymore. Even his own family had joined the enemy now. This wasn't just a hiccup in his plans, it was a mission-ending disaster. He might as well go back to Gluteus's villa and hand himself in.

"Look," said the soldier more kindly. "It's a long way back to town in the dark with an injured foot.

Why don't I see if there's a spare patch of straw in the stables for you to rest up for the night? Who knows, there might even be a dinner ration going spare if you're lucky. And then I'll sort you out with a lift tomorrow morning when the delivery carts head back. How does that sound?"

Oliver nodded, fighting back tears of frustration. It really *was* a kind offer and the best one they were going to get under the circumstances. Why couldn't anyone see what Dr Midnight was up to though? That was the bit that *really* got to him. Here he was, trying to save Roman Britain from the doctor's evil history-changing clutches and all anyone could say was how nice his beans were.

Just wait until you see the real *Dr Midnight*, he thought as the soldier helped Jules up onto his horse. *Wait until it's* your *friend locked up in his Chamber of Pain. Your toes he's feeding to his precious poodle. He might be all sweetness and light and toffee popcorn now, but just wait until he's got that Emperor's wreath on his head. There'll be no stopping him then…*

The soldier may have been blind to the Emperor-Midnight-shaped dangers ahead of them all, but he was as good as his word when it came to looking after them. He led them to a warm corner of the stables, with a bale of hay for Jules to rest her ankle on and some spare straw to snuggle down in. It was scratchy and smelly and rustled every time they moved, but it was a lot comfier than the cold, damp ground outside. He even sent over some hunks of bread once they were settled in, to ward off the worst of their hunger. It was all Oliver could do to force his down though – his appetite seemed to have disappeared along with the last traces of hope.

"Don't worry," said Jules, squeezing his hand as they lay there in the darkness, listening to the twitch and snort of the horses. "It's not over yet. We'll think of something."

But all Oliver could think of was his own bed at home. Of his mum and dad tucking in his empty sheets and kissing his cold pillow goodnight. Were they missing him already? Did they know what had happened? That the mission had failed and Oliver wasn't coming home again? Not ever?

Jules yawned, settling down with a final wriggle. "Things will look better in the morning, you'll see," she promised. "They always do."

CHAPTER XI

Jules was wrong. Things didn't look *any* better in the morning. Oliver was still trapped in the wrong century and the wrong pants, and now he had flea bites all the way up his legs as well. Still, at least scratching gave him something else to think about. Something other than Dr Midnight and the big cloud of doom hanging over their heads.

The soldier had arranged for them to travel back to town in the fish man's cart, which sounded like a good idea until they climbed on board. Stale snail milk and boar's blood was nothing compared to the stench of seafood. Whatever it was the fish man had been delivering for the fort commander's feast,

Oliver hoped it tasted better than it smelt.

"Poo-ee," said Jules, cheerfully. The swelling on her ankle had gone down overnight but she was still limping. She seemed in remarkably good spirits though, considering *her* plans were all in ruins too. "This smells even worse than you!"

Oliver couldn't even manage a smile, let alone a laugh. "What's it like then, being a slave?" he asked.

As far as he could see there were only two choices now – turn himself in to Dr Midnight and see out the rest of his days in the Chamber of Pain, or wait for Her Majesty's S Service to invent another time machine and send someone back to rescue him. But that might take weeks. Months even. And there'd be nothing left of him to rescue if he couldn't find a job and somewhere to stay.

"Why?" said Jules. "Why would you ask that?" She didn't seem quite so cheerful anymore. "Are you sending me back? Is that it?"

"No, of course not," Oliver told her. "It's just..."

Jules carried on as if he hadn't spoken. "You

don't know what it's like working for my master. He's a cruel man. Cruel and greedy. Trust me, he treats his animals better than he treats his slaves. And I'll be in so much trouble if I go back there now." She shuddered at the thought. "Please, Oliver. Please don't turn me in."

"Turn you in? Of course not. Why would you think that? I'm just working through my options, that's all."

What other options were there though? He and Jules couldn't exactly take on Dr Midnight's army of guards and old ladies on their own, could they? *That's it, drop your weapons everyone. Ditch the knitting needles and tie up that poodle or we'll release the fish stink...*

The rest of the journey back to town passed in worried silence. Oliver and Jules stayed hidden under a stinky sheet of cloth, hardly daring to breathe as they approached the drive-through burger bar. That's where Knitting Nora would have told the guards to look for them. Oliver crossed his fingers for luck as they clattered on past, ignoring the itch in his legs and the fishy tickle in his nose. But no one came chasing up the road after them, waving their swords and shouting for the cart to stop. They were safe. For now.

"What's happening? Are we there?" asked Oliver, as the cart slowed to a standstill.

Jules peeped out. "No, we're just stuck in traffic by the West Gate. It's always bad at this time of day." She stiffened suddenly. "Look at that," she hissed. "If you want to know what it's like being a slave, look down there." She pointed to a raggedy-looking boy on the pavement below, who stood quivering with fear before his master's raised stick.

"I told you I wanted *fresh* oysters, you fool," roared his red-faced master. "Now get back to the market and fetch me some better ones before I beat you back there myself." He brought his cane down on the poor boy's legs with a nasty thwack. "And you'd better get it right this time or I'll…"

The cart rumbled on before they could hear any

more.

"Wait, was that him?" asked Oliver, noticing his friend's pale face and trembling hands. "Was that your master?"

"No," said Jules, dragging him back down onto the floor of the cart and pulling the fishy sheet over their heads again. "My master's *much* worse than that. His house is five streets down from here – the big white one on the corner. I can't show you though – it's too risky." She clutched at Oliver's arm. "But *now* you see why I can't go back to him. There's got to be another way. There must be."

"Alright. Let's try and find the fast food man," Oliver suggested. "At least we know *he's* not working for Dr Midnight. Maybe he'll have an idea."

Jules nodded. "Or a sausage," she said, looking happier already.

The cart set them down near the forum – a large market square surrounded by covered walkways and important-looking buildings – and they thanked the fish man for the lift.

"You're welcome," he said. "Sorry I can't take you any further but I've got to get ready for my appointment. I'm meeting the owner of Burger Emperor to discuss a new line of fish finger sandwiches. Me!" he said, preening like a peacock. "Going into business with the emperor of fast food! Fingers crossed, anyway… fish fingers that is! Wish me luck."

Huh! It wasn't luck he needed, it was sense – enough sense to see Dr Midnight for what he really was. Oliver thought about warning him – *don't go, that man's nothing but trouble* – but what was the point? He wouldn't listen anyway. No one listened.

"Good luck," he said, instead. "We'd better be going too. We've got an important appointment at the… at the…" He tried to think of somewhere far away to throw any followers off the scent. Because if the fish man got talking about the scruffy-looking pair he'd just given a lift to, Dr Midnight might put two and two together. "At the amphitheatre. Yes, that's right. We've got an important appointment with one of the gladiators. Gary, I think his name is. Gary Garricus the Gladiator. Thanks again for the lift, anyway."

"Gary? What kind of a name is Gary?" scoffed Jules, as they skirted past a team of slaves in the process of removing a statue from its plinth.

"It was the best I could think of in a hurry," said Oliver, wondering what was going on. It looked like a statue of Mercury, judging by the winged sandals, but why would anyone want to take *that* down?

"Oof," grunted the nearest slave, mopping his brow on a roll of parchment. "Why couldn't he just have built his statue *next* to this one instead?"

"Shh," said a second slave. "You can't go around saying things like that. His spies are everywhere."

"Whose spies?" asked Oliver, although he had a nasty feeling he already knew the answer to that one.

"This chap here," said the first slave, unrolling his parchment to show Oliver the plans. It was a statue of a short, bald man with an evil smile and a giant tin of baked beans. An equally evil-looking poodle sat at his feet, her sharp teeth bared for battle.

"He's got a whole team of the finest marble-carvers chipping away as we speak," said the slave. "And if this old statue isn't gone by the time they've finished…" He pulled a finger across his neck and gulped.

"I'd better let you get back to it then," said Oliver, who couldn't think of anything worse to find in the middle of the forum than a marble copy of Dr Midnight.

He and Jules hurried on through the impressive archway into the busy grid of streets beyond. Oliver was hopelessly lost within minutes – the town seemed even busier than yesterday and the streets all looked the same – but fortunately Jules remembered the way.

"It should be down here," she finally announced, turning onto a road that looked exactly like the one they'd just left. "I wonder if he's started cooking yet… Come on, hurry up." She headed off down the street at an impressive hobble, spurred on by the thought of hot meat. But breakfast would have to wait, Oliver realised, as a dark shadow fell across the road. A whole crowd of dark shadows. *Uh-oh…*

"There he is!" shouted an angry-looking guard. "That's the one we're looking for. Get him!"

"Quick, hide," Oliver told Jules, pushing her into a nearby doorway. "It's me they're looking for. I'll come and find you once I've shaken them off."

"Head for the baths," she suggested, pointing back the way they'd just come, "and try and give them the slip. Everyone looks the same without their clothes on."

It was a good idea – or at least it would have been if he knew where the baths were – but there was no time to ask for directions. Oliver was already off, sprinting back up the street with the gang of guards clattering after him. Which way now? He headed for the biggest crowd he could find, ducking and weaving around jabbing elbows, leaping over legs and feet like a hurdler. Angry voices yelled at him as he tore past.

"Oi! Watch it."

"Hey, slow down!"

"Mind where you're going."

"Look at the state of your tunic. You wanna get some Brutus Urine-Rinse on that."

"Get him!" roared the guards, drawing closer and closer. "Stop that boy!"

Somehow Oliver's wild flight had led him straight to the baths. There they were, just up ahead. Thank goodness for that! He bounded up the steps into the great bath house, hoping Jules was right. Hoping he'd be able to throw his pursuers off the scent amongst the billowing steam of the hot room – the Caldarium – or by holding his breath at the bottom of the chilly Frigidarium pool. And he'd be twice as hard to spot by then, without his blood-stained tunic to give him away.

There was only one problem. Oliver had been expecting the other bathers to be naked – just like in the library book he'd borrowed for his project. But he'd forgotten about Dr Midnight and his swimming trunks. And without a pair of his own, he'd stick out like a sore thumb (like a bare bum, even). He hurried on into the changing room, desperately hoping to find a spare pair he could borrow. It looked exactly like the picture in the library book, with long benches running along the walls and high shelves where people could leave their clothes and sandals. But no sign of any trunks.

Time was running out. Oliver could hear the guards shouting behind him as they charged through the baths into the Caldarium. He heard them clattering into the private rooms, yelling at the oil-covered rich men being scraped clean by their slaves.

"You seen a scruffy little urchin in a ripped tunic?" they asked.

"You seen a runaway pipsqueak with blood all over his clothes?"

He was right – it was his outfit that was the giveaway. Oliver kicked off his sandals and wriggled out of his tunic, grabbing a replacement one from the shelf by his head. He threw it on and snatched up a nearby towel as the guards burst into the changing room, sharp swords at the ready.

Gulp! Oliver kept his face hidden from view as he pretended to dry his hair. His throat had gone all dry and his legs were trembling like crazy under the borrowed tunic. This was it. They had him now...

"You seen a funny-looking boy in a blood-stained tunic?" asked one of the guards, pointing at Oliver with the gleaming tip of his blade.

Oliver shook his head, mumbling into his towel with as deep a voice as he could manage. "No, no. Definitely not. Sorry."

"Really? He's blonde and weedy, with bite marks on his ankle."

Who was he calling weedy? Oliver shook his head again, shuffling one leg behind the other. "I'd remember if I had," he grunted. "Maybe he went to the amphitheatre instead."

"Well it doesn't look like he's here," piped up

another guard. "You *sure* he came into the baths, Marcus?"

Marcus, a short fat man with sticky-out ears, shrugged his shoulders. "I don't know. It was busy. Maybe I made a mistake."

"Made a mistake? You know what happened to the last fella who did that. Dr Midnight doesn't like mistakes."

Marcus shivered.

"Well don't just stand there then," said the first guard. "If he's not in the baths, we'd better get back out there and find him... before Dr Midnight finds us."

Oliver held his breath as they clomped their way back out of the changing room. The noise of their nail-studded sandals grew fainter and fainter until finally it disappeared altogether. *Phew!* He'd done it – he was safe. Or so he thought.

CHAPTER XII

"Oi, that's my tunic," came a gruff voice from the doorway.

"What? I mean, pardon?" Oliver turned to see an angry-looking man with one long eyebrow stretching all the way across his face.

"I *said* that's my tunic you're wearing." Eyebrow glared at him. "I'd recognise that blob of fish sauce anywhere. Come here, you little thief."

"No, no. I wasn't stealing it, I swear. Just borrowing it for a bit," said Oliver, trying to remember what the punishment for theft was in Roman times. A fine? A whipping? "It was an emergency…"

Eyebrow made a funny growling noise in his throat, like Josephine getting ready to attack. He looked angrier than ever.

"Here," said Oliver, slipping off the tunic and holding it out to him. "Have it back. I'm really sorry."

But the man just stood there, his long eyebrow furrowed in confusion. "What *are* you wearing?" he asked at last, pointing to Mrs Starling's frilly knickers.

"Er... erm... these? They're gladiator pants," Oliver said, thinking quickly. The heat from his blushing cheeks could have warmed up half the pools in the bath house. "They're a bit like a loincloth but better for fighting in... *All* the gladiators wear pants like these where I come from."

"You?" Eyebrow laughed. "A gladiator? You're too tiny to fight anyone. And who's that lady on the back?"

"That's the Queen," Oliver said. "Er... I mean Juno. Queen of all the gods and goddesses. Anyway,

I really must be going – my friend will be waiting for me. Sorry again about the tunic mix-up."

He struggled back into his own blood-smeared clothes, hoping the man would believe him. Hoping he wouldn't drag him away for stealing, or tell Dr Midnight's guards he'd found the boy they were looking for... *Thud!* The mini history book slipped out of his tunic onto the changing room floor.

Eyebrow lunged for it, like a cat pouncing on a mouse. "What's this then?"

"Er..." Oliver gulped, trying to think of a sensible answer that didn't involve secret agents or time travel. Or knickers. "It's a book," he said at last. Perhaps it was best to keep things simple. "They're very popular where I come from."

"A book? Never heard of it. What does it do?"

"It's sort of like a scroll," Oliver explained, "but instead of having to roll the paper out you turn the pages, like this. See? And they can be about anything – magic, adventure, love – anything at all. This one's more of a text book than a story though.

A bit like the ones we use at school."

"School, did you say?" Eyebrow grabbed Oliver by the ear. "School? I knew it! You're not a gladiator at all, are you? You're just a schoolboy. A runaway schoolboy *and* a thief. Let's see what your teacher has to say about *that*, shall we?"

What? Oliver would have given anything to be back at school, in proper school uniform, learning about history instead of living it. But as for school in Roman Britain... that was a different matter altogether. Having to learn every lesson by heart (with beatings if you forgot them) didn't seem like much fun at all.

"I think you'd better come with me, young man," said Eyebrow, yanking Oliver along by his ear.

"Hey, get off. That hurts!"

Eyebrow took no notice, dragging him across the changing room, like a dog on a lead, and back out through the baths into the sunshine. He seemed to have forgotten all about his tunic, marching along in his swimming trunks with his hairy belly on proud display. They must have made a funny-looking pair but Oliver was too sore and scared to even *think* about laughing.

Ow, ow, ow, ow, owwwwww! Oliver broke into a stumbling jog as they charged down the steps onto the busy street below, his stretched ear throbbing with pain. If the man tugged any harder he'd pull it off altogether! On the plus side, it might be a good disguise, given that Dr Midnight's guards were looking for a boy with *two* ears. But on the downside (and it was quite a big downside, all things considered), he'd only have one ear.

"Oliver, wait," came a breathless cry from behind. Jules! "Wait for me."

Oliver turned to see – or at least he tried to – forgetting, for a millisecond, about the pincer-like grip on his poor lobe. He yelped in agony as the tug on his ear doubled.

"Please," he begged. "Let go of me. I need to tell my friend what's happening. She'll be worried."

"I'll let go of you when we get there," said

Eyebrow, his grip as tight as ever. But he did slow down, at least, giving Jules time to catch up.

"Hands off my friend," she gasped, breathless from her high-speed hobble. "Do you work for Dr Midnight too? Are you one of his Knitty Noras?"

"Huh?" Eyebrow couldn't have looked more puzzled if he tried. "Who are you calling nitty?"

"Where are you taking him?" asked Jules, without waiting for an answer. "Back to the Chamber of Pain?"

Eyebrow chuckled to himself. "So that's what they're calling it these days, is it? Yes," he told her, giving Oliver's ear an extra yank. "I'm taking this little runaway back to school where he belongs."

"School?" Jules's eyes widened. She looked positively excited by the idea. "In that case I'm a runaway too… a runaway schoolboy that is. Can I come?"

"If you insist," said Eyebrow, grabbing hold of her ear with his other hand. "Funniest-looking schoolboy *I* ever saw but it takes all sorts, I guess."

"It certainly does," agreed Jules. "Aren't you cold without any clothes on?"

School, when they finally arrived (having gone all the way back to the baths for Eyebrow's forgotten tunic), turned out to be a single room off the street with a curtain across the doorway. No playground. No cheery displays on the wall. No sign of anything fun at all. The Roman children sat on stools, clutching wax-spread wooden boards, with pointed sticks for scratching out words and figures. And at the front of the room sat a thin, weary-looking man who reminded Oliver of his old headmaster, Mr Steadfast. They had the same watery blue eyes and furrowed brow, the same look of dull exhaustion. Perhaps Roman teachers weren't so different after all, he thought hopefully, before he noticed the long wooden cane resting against his leg. *Eek!*

"Do these tearaways belong to you, Educo?" asked Eyebrow, giving Oliver and Jules a gentle shove.

Educo Constantis, the schoolmaster, glanced up.

He peered at them for a few moments and then shrugged. "Oh, I don't know," he said. "They all look the same to me. My poor eyes aren't what they were. Come in, come in. You're just in time for our mathematics assessment."

A maths test? Oliver's heart sank. Was there no escape?

"Where are your wax tablets then?" asked Educo, squinting at their empty hands. "You won't get very far without them, will you?"

Oliver didn't know what to say. "We er... We must have left them at the library..." Yes. He seemed to remember something about the Romans bringing libraries to Britain. And rabbits. And turnips...

"What's that you say?" muttered the schoolmaster, cupping a hand to his ear. "Something about bribery? You'll have to speak up, boy. My ears aren't what they were either."

My ear's seen better days too, thought Oliver, his poor reddened lobe still pulsing with pain.

"Oh never mind," said Educo, handing them a sharpened twig each and pointing to some empty chairs. "You'll have to share with your neighbours. Of course, strictly speaking, I should be beating any latecomers..." He picked up his cane, fixing them with a mean stare.

Oliver took a few steps back. Nothing like this ever happened at *his* school. Mrs Rudderson never beat anyone for missing registration.

"...But that will only delay the rest of the class," finished the schoolmaster, wearily. "Just sit down for now."

Oliver breathed a silent sigh of relief and found a spare stool next to a skinny boy with a bony chin. Jules took the stool to his left, grinning at Oliver as they sat down, her eyes gleaming with excitement. Apart from that first bite of sausage the day before, he'd never seen her looking so happy.

"But be warned," continued Educo. "I shall take a very dim view of anyone who has not learnt their mathematics to my satisfaction." He banged the floor with his cane, making everyone jump. "Right then. From the top. Five multiplied by thirty-five."

"Okay," muttered Oliver under his breath, pulling his stool closer to his neighbour's wax board. "Stay calm. You can do this."

He scratched the sum into the surface of the wax, wishing he had a proper pencil and paper, and got to work with his calculations. One hundred and seventy-five. Did that sound right? He stole a quick glance at his neighbour's efforts – just to check he hadn't done anything stupid – and got a nasty shock.

Even if it *was* the right answer it was still written all wrong. For a Roman maths test he needed Roman numerals, didn't he? If only Florence was here, with that Roman numeral ruler she'd bought at the museum on their school trip. *She'd* know what the answers were and she'd have been happy to share them with him too. Unlike Bony Chin, who covered them up with his other hand when he caught him peeking.

Oliver cracked his knuckles and racked his

brains, trying to think back to his school project. Romans numbers were all Is and Xs and Vs, weren't they? And Cs. Yes, C was a hundred – that was right. Ten was X and five was V. And fifty, what was that? L? Yes, that rang a bell… which would make the answer CLXXV. But by the time he'd finally worked out *that* question, the schoolmaster was already onto number four.

By the end of the test, Oliver had answered a grand total of six questions. His brain hurt almost as much as his ear, and his wrist ached from the effort of scratching into the wax. He stole another quick glance at his neighbour's work to find that Bony Chin had three or four times as many answers as him. No prizes for guessing which of his pupils Educo would be turning his horrible cane on… Maybe he and Jules should make a run for it while they still had the chance. Surely Eyebrow would be gone by now? But Jules was still smiling away to herself, as if maths tests were some kind of wonderful treat. As if school was the best thing that had ever happened to her.

"Right then," said Educo, swishing the cane backwards and forwards through the air. "You, boy!" He pointed at Jules. "Stand up. You can do the first five to start us off."

Jules shook her head. "Sorry, sir," she said. "I can't remember what the questions were now. I didn't write anything down because... well, because I don't know how to read or write. All I've got here is a picture of Knitty Nora and a sausage." She held up the wax tablet to show him. "I know that fourteen times seventy-eight equals one thousand and ninety-two though. Does that help? And twenty-three multiplied by fifty-six is one thousand, two hundred and eighty-eight..."

"What do you mean, you don't know how to read and write?" barked Educo, beckoning her to the front of the class. "You're not a schoolboy at all, are you?" he said, peering at her face. "Wait a minute, you're not even a boy!"

CHAPTER XIII

Uh-oh. Jules was in trouble now. Big trouble.

"I'm sorry," she said.

Oliver shifted in his seat, getting ready to run. The moment Educo reached for his cane they'd be out of there. But Jules hadn't finished yet.

"You're right," she admitted, "I'm not a boy at all – just a girl with a bad haircut." She pulled back her shoulders and carried on bravely. "It's tricky cutting it yourself without a mirror though."

Oh yes, she was brave all right. Brave enough to escape from her cruel master in the first place. Brave enough to climb down a bit of wool in the middle of a storm. Brave enough to stand up there in front of the scariest teacher ever, discussing haircuts.

"But I'd give anything for a place in your school," she told Educo, "once I've helped Oliver get back to Gobblefrog. I'll sweep your floors, cook your dinner, scrub your clothes, polish your cane, re-wax your tablets…" She paused to catch her breath. "And as soon as I've learnt to read I can help with that too. My eyesight's good enough for the two of us."

Educo stared at her in silence, his wrinkled upper lip twitching like a startled grub. The rest of the class held its breath and waited.

"Ridiculous," he said at last. "I've never *heard* such a preposterous plan. And yet…" He scratched his chin and sighed. "I *could* do with a bit of help around the place, that's for certain. I'm not getting any younger and I can't afford a new slave on my wages…"

"I make very tasty honey cakes, too," said Jules. "And barley soup."

"Honey cakes, eh?" Educo nodded gruffly.

"Alright," he agreed. "You've got yourself a deal. Sit back down for now though while we finish off this test."

Oliver grinned to himself. Some good news, at last! That was a *much* better plan than smuggling Jules back to the future with him. He wasn't sure how she'd have managed in a world of cars and computers and electricity.

"Don't worry about helping me get home," he whispered, as she took her seat again. "I'll find a way, somehow. This is too good an opportunity for you to miss. I've never known anyone do maths sums like that in their head!"

"No," said Jules. "I'm still going to help you free your friend and rescue that time machine. School will just have to wait a bit longer. I can't let you do this on your own."

"You, boy," interrupted Educo, pointing his cane at Oliver. "You can give us the answers instead."

Oliver's smile faded as he dragged himself onto his feet, trying to decide what to do. Stay put and hope for the best, or run?

"Come on," said the schoolmaster. "We're waiting…" He paused, turning towards the doorway as someone pulled the curtain aside. "Not *another* interruption," he grumbled. "What now?"

Oliver looked up hopefully. Maybe Eyebrow had realised he wasn't a Roman schoolboy after all and come to take him back again. Another round of ear-dragging was better than a maths test beating with that big nasty cane. Only it wasn't Eyebrow at all. It was Owl.

Oliver had never been so glad to see anyone in his entire life.

"Ha! Found you!" said Owl. "So *this* is where you've been hiding, is it, you lousy little good-for-nothing?" He turned to Educo. "The boy's a wicked, useless slave. Never does what he's told. Always running off and getting into mischief. I do apologise."

"I *thought* he looked like trouble," said Educo, pointing his cane at Oliver.

"Come now, boy," said Owl, with a sly wink. "School's no place for the likes of you."

Oliver winked back. "That's him," he whispered to Jules. "That's my friend, Owl. Everything's going to be okay now, which means you can stay here and start your new life at school."

"Alright," she finally agreed. "If you're sure. I'm going to miss you though. Good luck with Dr Midnight and the Noras. And thanks for sharing your sausage."

"I'm going to miss you too," said Oliver. "Good luck with the grumpy schoolteacher. And thanks for being my friend. I'd have been lost without you."

"Hurry up, boy," said Owl. "We haven't got all day, you know."

"Of course, master. Sorry, master. Just coming." Oliver handed in his wax-scraping stick, waved goodbye to Jules, and dashed for the door before anyone could stop him.

"Thank goodness," he gasped, high-fiving Agent Owl as the curtain closed behind them. "I didn't know what had happened to you. I thought you'd been captured by Dr Midnight."

"I had," said Owl, looking pleased with himself. "I spent all night in his Chamber of Pain having my toes pricked with a giant nappy pin. It's not actually as painful as you'd think. But as soon as the guard in charge of toe-pricking went to have his breakfast I swung into action with a little trick I like to call the 'key under the door sliparoo'."

"What?" Oliver didn't even know what a *normal* sliparoo was, let alone a key under the door one. "I mean, pardon? Is that a special secret agent thing?"

"It's actually something I learnt from an old children's book," Owl admitted, sheepishly. "Luckily for me there was a nice big gap under the door, and the dopey guard had forgotten to take the key out of the lock. It was a proper key too, like the Portaloo one round Dr Midnight's neck, not one of those funny Roman ones. So I slid the end of my toga under the gap and wiggled the key back out the hole with my little finger onto the waiting material.

Clever, huh? All I had to do then was pull it back underneath the door and bingo!"

"Wow, that's brilliant!" said Oliver, relief still flooding through his body. Thank goodness they'd found each other again.

Owl grinned. "And after *that* it was simply a matter of dodging the guards, wrestling my leg from Josephine's mouth, knocking Dr Midnight out with a half-eaten boar's head I found lying around, and locking him up in his own Chamber of Pain." He held up a big metal key. "And he won't be getting out of *there* in a hurry without this."

"But how did you know where to find me?" asked Oliver. "I've been all the way out to the fort and back looking for my great-great-great-great-more-greats-than-we've-got-time-for-great-grandfather."

Owl looked impressed.

"I didn't," he said. "But I heard a group of guards heading off to town to search for you this morning, so I guessed that's where you'd be. I hitched a lift in and searched every street, shop and doorway until I found you. Simple! And here I am – not a moment too soon by the looks of it. Have you eaten? I found these in the kitchen on my way out."

He held up a handful of milk-soaked snails.

"It's okay," said Oliver, quickly. "I'm still full from my bit of bread last night. I *was* going back to see the sausage man with my new Roman friend, Jules, but then I got chased by Dr Midnight's guards and dragged off to school by a man at the baths."

"My, my, you have been busy."

"And I was coming back to rescue you," said Oliver, "I promise. As soon as I thought of a proper plan… The Titus Stabbicus one didn't work out very well, unfortunately. He's on Dr Midnight's side now, like everyone else."

"I'm just glad you got away when you did," said Owl. "Top work, Agent Starling. But now that we've seen the full extent of Dr Midnight's fiendish plans for ourselves, I think it's time we put a stop to them. Agreed?"

"Agreed," agreed Oliver. "And you've done the hard catching-him bit already. Now we just have to rescue the photo booth and take Dr M back to the future, where he belongs. Future jail, that is."

"Plus a quick trip back to three weeks ago last Tuesday," Owl pointed out, "to stop him arriving in the first place. Then history can finally go back to normal."

Oliver nodded. "No more baked beans and ride-through burger bars. No more bendy roads and nappy pin birthday badges. No more swimming trunks. And no more Emperor Midnight."

Take that, *World's Number One Evil Genius. No one messes with her Majesty's S Service and gets away with it.* But if *everything* in the last three weeks got cancelled out, Oliver suddenly realised, there'd be no meeting Jules either. Where would that leave her? He'd have to try and think of a way round that one.

Owl looked thoughtful too. "Hmm. It's a pity I didn't think this through earlier. It's all a bit new to me," he admitted, "this time travel stuff. If only we'd gone straight back to three weeks ago last Tuesday in the first place, we could have saved ourselves a lot of trouble and toe-pricks. But then on the other hand we'd never have seen all this, would we?" He gestured down the street towards a familiar-looking ginger cat, chasing a scrap of parchment over the cobbles. "And we'd never have got to try real-life Roman snails." He popped one into his mouth – shell and all – and crunched down hard.

"Ew, yuck," he said, spitting it out again. "On second thoughts *don't* try the real-life Roman snails. Not the raw ones anyway. Maybe we'll find something nicer back at the villa."

"To the villa!" cried Oliver, setting off up the street with fresh determination.

"Agent Starling?" called Owl.

"Yes?"

"Much as I admire your enthusiasm, there's just one problem."

"What?" asked Oliver. "I mean, pardon. Wait, no I don't, I mean 'what'. What is it?"

Owl grinned, his lips glistening with snail juice. "You're going the wrong way," he said.

CHAPTER XIV

Oliver and Owl kept a sharp lookout as they went, anxious to avoid Dr Midnight's guards, but their luck seemed to be holding. Soon they were back on the open road, heading past the cemetery and out into the countryside. Oliver felt more hopeful than he had since they arrived. The worst bits of the mission were behind them now and soon Roman Britain would be behind them too.

This time tomorrow, he'd be back in the twenty-first century enjoying all the comforts of modern life. Hooray for trousers and trainers! Three cheers for flushing loos and toilet roll! Hooray for cane-less school and non-snaily dinners! In fact, if their plan worked, he should be back in time for dinner tonight… for creamy chicken risotto topped with mountains of melted cheese. There might even be apple pie for pudding seeing as it was a special occasion. After all, it wasn't every day a Starling got to save the history of the world from an evil genius. His mum made the best apple pies ever, with thick melt-in-the-mouth pastry and tangy chunks of apple smothered in vanilla ice cream. Maybe he could invite Florence over too. It felt like years since he'd last seen her. Hundreds and hundreds of years.

"Mmmmm," murmured Oliver, picturing a large scoop of vanilla melting down the warm pastry crust. And another, slightly smaller scoop, melting down his warm pastry-covered chin… He could practically taste it now.

"Sorry, what was that?" asked Owl.

"I was just thinking about Mum's apple pie," he explained. "It would be good if we could make it home in time for dinner tonight."

"Of course we can," said Owl, with a grin. "Once

we get our time machine back we can make it home for dinner any day you want. We could go and have Christmas dinner three years ago if that's what you fancy. I might pass on the Brussels sprouts and cranberry sauce myself... but we can discuss menus once we've taken care of Dr Midnight."

Back at the villa, the first lot of guards had finally given up the search for their lost prisoners and were lying on the lawn in a state of exhaustion. And there – in the middle of the garden – stood Gluteus and the photo booth.

"Hmmm," said Owl, peeping out from behind a pillar. "This might be trickier than I thought. Even with Dr Midnight safely locked away we're still outnumbered." He counted up the guards under his breath and sighed. "And we need a plan to get Gluteus out of the way too... I can't believe he's *still* taking photos of himself."

"Maybe we could lure him away with something to eat?" Oliver suggested, his own stomach growling with hunger. He'd lied about being full up from last night's bread. "It must be nearly lunchtime by now."

Owl stroked his missing beard. "Good thinking, Agent Starling. These Romans certainly like their food, don't they? Did you see all those pigeons and honey cakes in the kitchen? All those roasted dormice and peacock eggs? They must spend all day on their bottoms, just eating."

"Not on their bottoms, they don't," said Oliver, thinking back to his history project. "Rich Romans, like Gluteus, eat their meals lying down."

Owl raised his eyebrows. "Lying down for dinner? Utterly ridiculous. Mind you, I never say 'no' to biscuits in bed. Especially custard creams… but that's different. Biscuits in bed is what puts the Great in Great Britain. It's what puts the Hope in the Land of Hope and Glory. It's what puts the crumbs in my freshly ironed sheets…" He trailed off, with a faraway biscuity look in his eyes.

Oliver coughed.

"Ah yes," said Owl. "Where were we?"

"On the way to the kitchens for some food?"

suggested Oliver hopefully.

"Wrong," came a low growl from behind. "You were on the way to your DOOM!"

"Dr Midnight!" cried the secret agents in horror. But it was too late to run. The guards had already sprung into action at the sound of his voice, rushing to their master's aid. Two strong arms grabbed Oliver around the chest in a tight bear hug, lifting him clean off the ground.

"Oh great," said Owl, as two more arms grabbed him in a matching bear hug of his own. "Just when everything was going so well."

"Now then," said Dr Midnight, rubbing the boar-shaped bump on his forehead, "this is nice, isn't it? All of us together again?" He laughed a suitably evil laugh, leaning in close to Owl's face. "Thought you could lock me up in my own Chamber of Pain, did you, Owly-pants? Thought you could sneak off with your time machine and foil my dastardly plans? Ha!" He cackled a suitably evil cackle.

"I did actually, yes," admitted Owl. "How did

you manage it? How did you get out of a locked cell without a key?"

"One word," said Dr Midnight, looking smug. "Knitting needle."

"That's two words, actually," Oliver pointed out but Dr Midnight wasn't listening. He was too busy revelling in his not-so-daring escape.

"There's more to an army of old lady spies than mere poodle coats, you know," he crowed. "There's no lock on the planet those ladies can't pick with their needles." He paused, scratching at his bald head for inspiration. "You've interrupted my train of thought now. Where was I up to with my evil genius victory boast?"

"You'd just finished the cackling bit," said Oliver, helpfully.

"Ah yes, that's it. Thank you. Thought you'd head back in time until just before I arrived, did you? Make sure you were lying in wait for me when I first got here... was *that* your cunning plan? Ha!" Dr Midnight said again. "I knew it. Not as stupid as

I look, eh?"

"No one could be as stupid as *you* look," said Owl.

"That's enough! Guards! Take them away. And there'll be no keys under the door this time, thank you very much," said Dr Midnight. "No, I've got big plans for you both. And I mean seriously big. Bigger than Big Ben big."

Owl whistled. "Gosh. That really *is* big."

"Word is there'll be some rather fierce lions from Africa starring at the gladiatorial games tomorrow. And who better to fight them than a pair of meddling secret agents who don't know when to mind their own business?" Dr Midnight smiled a suitably evil smile, with a big bit of snail meat stuck between his front teeth. "I think I'll get myself one of those tubs of popcorn I've been selling and sit back and enjoy the show. There now," he said to Oliver, "doesn't that sound fun? I *do* hope you like cats... I hear these ones are rather hungry..."

CHAPTER XV

Oliver and Owl were dragged away to a tiny room with bare walls and thick metal bars across the window.

"Is this it?" said Oliver. "Is this the Chamber of Pain?"

Owl shook his head. "No. There'll be no nappy pin toe pricks for us, I'm afraid. I don't know *where* we are now. But at least there's a good view. That's something, I suppose."

Oliver stood on tiptoe and peered out through the bars. There were the villa gardens, where they'd been captured twice in two days, and there was the road stretching off towards the town in the far distance. And somewhere, just outside that town stood the amphitheatre, with its popcorn stall and horrible hungry lions. His eyes filled with tears as he thought about the meal they'd be enjoying tomorrow. What chance would an eleven-year-old boy in frilly knickers have against a killer cat?

"Don't worry," said Owl. "I'll find a way out of this. I always do."

Oliver wiped his eyes and tried to smile. He wanted to believe him, he really did, but he'd never been less certain of anything in his life. He'd spent all morning telling people he was off to the amphitheatre, trying to throw them off the scent, and now he really was. It would have been funny if it wasn't so terrifying. Where was Gary the Gladiator when he needed him?

"Just think of all the stories you'll be able to tell your friends when you get back home," Owl said, trying to cheer him up.

"*If* I get back home." Home was hundreds and hundreds of years away. And so was Florence. The only way he'd get to share his adventures with her now was by chipping them into a bit of stone for archaeologists to discover in the distant future. And there wouldn't be much time for that with a hungry lion chasing after him.

"Of course you will," said Owl. "I promised your mum and dad I'd bring you back safe and sound, didn't I? And I always keep my promises. Scout's honour."

Oliver scratched his flea bites and sighed. His mum and dad hadn't even been born yet. Queen Victoria hadn't been born. Nor had Shakespeare. Even William the Conqueror hadn't put in an appearance yet.

"I expect your mum's out shopping for a new hat as we speak," said Owl. "She'll be needing something smart for when she meets the Queen. Between you and me, I'm not sure the whole tiara and bunting look was really working."

"Have *you* ever met the Queen?" asked Oliver. He'd rather be thinking about crowns and corgis than sharp lion teeth and razor cat claws.

"Have *I* met the Queen?" said Owl with a grin. "Have *I* met the Queen?! Why, my dear boy, the Queen is one of my oldest friends. Do you know, she keeps a spare pair of slippers at Buckingham Palace for me to wear when I'm visiting? And sometimes, if we've stayed up very late talking or playing Monopoly, I borrow a pair of royal pyjamas too and stay over at the palace. That's quite a treat I can tell you – Buckingham breakfasts are out of this world… fantastic fried eggs. I'll have to take you some day."

Oliver tried to picture it… Owl in his dark glasses and funny false beard fighting over Mayfair and Park Lane with Her Majesty. Were you still allowed to charge her rent if she landed on your houses and hotels? Did she have a special royal 'get out of jail free' card?

"One time," Owl laughed, "we spent all morning eating breakfast. I had five helpings. By the time we'd finished, it was lunchtime."

"And what does the Queen eat for lunch?"

"Cheese and pickle sandwiches mainly. Or sardines on toast at the weekend."

It was a good job Mrs Starling didn't know that, Oliver thought, otherwise *they'd* be having sardines every Saturday and Sunday too. "And what about dinner? Does she like risotto?"

"I'll have to ask her," said Owl. "But I know she likes sausages and mash – that's her favourite. With royal jelly for afters."

"And what's her favourite drink?"

"Earl Grey tea."

"Favourite colour?"

"That's easy – royal blue."

"Favourite film?"

"The King's Speech…"

The afternoon drifted by. Oliver was so busy listening to Owl's tales of life at the palace, followed by tales of his S Service adventures, that he forgot about feeling miserable and scared. He forgot about his flea bites (apart from the odd itchy tingle between stories) and the smell of his tunic. And he forgot that he was a prisoner again, centuries and centuries away from home. He even managed to forget about the lions.

Owl was halfway through a story about Agent Gorilla's granny and a gang of diamond smugglers when a key turned in the lock, making them both jump. The door was flung open by a mean-looking guard, with two more stationed behind him in case they tried to escape.

"Dinner time," announced Guard Number One. "Dr Midnight says you'll need some proper leftovers inside you tonight if you're going to be fighting lions tomorrow."

"Ooh, lovely," said Owl, cheerfully. "As long as it's not snails."

"Nope, they're all out of snails. It's cold baked beans and honey-coated dormice."

"Ew, lovely," said Owl, rather less cheerfully.

"And there's water in the jug," barked the guard, setting it down on the floor. "Enjoy."

"One more thing before you go," said Owl. "I've been having a bit of trouble with my er..." He looked embarrassed. "With my loincloth. It keeps coming undone. I was wondering if I could borrow a pin like yours." He pointed to the guard's nappy pin, which was fixed below his shoulder like an ornamental brooch. "I'd hate for anything to unravel in the middle of the games tomorrow. Be a bit embarrassing in front of everyone, and I certainly don't want to be tripping over it, do I?"

"Oh no you don't." The guard shook his head. "Dr Midnight warned us about you. He said you'd probably try and trick us into letting you go and we weren't to listen to a word you said."

"Of course," said Owl. "You've got your orders. I'm just thinking of the audience tomorrow, that's all. If I fall over, and get eaten by the lion straight away, it's not much of a show, is it? Surely it'll be better for Dr Midnight's popcorn sales if I spin it out a bit longer... you know, run around the arena a few times first, put up a bit of a fight. Nothing like watching gladiator-chasing to work up an appetite, is there?"

"Hmm." The guard looked worried. "I don't know…"

"I mean, where's the harm?" Owl smiled. "It's not as if I'm going to take on three big strong men like you with a little pin! I wouldn't stand a chance, would I?"

"Yeah," laughed the other two guards. "What's he going to do, toe-prick his way out?!"

The first guard grinned sheepishly. "Oh, go on then. I guess it can't do any harm." He undid the nappy pin and handed it to Owl. "Plenty more where that came from."

"Can I have one too, in that case?" asked Oliver. "My pants have been falling down since I got here."

"Yes, we know," said the second guard. "We've been getting regular underwear updates from the old ladies on that walkie talkie thingamajig. Here – you can have mine. Watch where you're putting that pin though!"

"Right, we're off. Eat up," said the third guard. "Big day tomorrow, eh?" He let out a lion's roar and they all fell about laughing as the door shut behind them.

Oliver could still hear them as they double-checked the lock:

"Don't forget to take the key out afterwards. You know what happened to the last fella who did that..."

"I heard he's on dog-walking duty for the next month."

"I heard he's picking up dog poo for the next year."

"I heard they turned him into dog food... poodle noodles!"

The laughter carried on all the way back down the corridor.

"Dormouse?" asked Owl, holding up a sticky brown lump covered in poppy seeds. It looked about as tasty as a toffee-coated slug. Oliver took the teeniest, tiniest nibble – he was so hungry he'd try anything – but it wasn't as bad as he thought. It tasted a bit like chicken, really. He tried another bite and then another.

"Mmm, it's quite nice actually," he said at last. "For a mouse."

"I'll take your word for it," said Owl. "I think I'll stick to the baked beans."

They ate in silence, both lost in their own thoughts.

"Why *do* you wear that funny fake beard you had on yesterday?" asked Oliver at last. "Why don't you just grow your own?"

"It's part of my cunning secret agent disguise," said Owl, handing him another dormouse. "Although I suppose if I did grow a real one I could strap a false chin on over the top… that might work." He smiled. "You're full of questions today aren't you?"

It was true. Oliver would rather be thinking of questions than cats. But there was no avoiding the lions when it came to his next one. "Do you think lions like dormice?" he asked. "I could smuggle some of these spare ones into the amphitheatre tomorrow to distract them, like I did with Josephine and the boar's head."

"Good thinking," said Owl, slurping up the last of the beans and pinning his nappy pin to the inside of his toga. "It might buy us some more time. But really Oliver, you mustn't worry, I've got a cunning plan. There's always a plan."

CHAPTER XVI

Oliver felt tired next morning – tired, aching and terrified. He'd spent an uncomfortable night on the stone floor (it was even worse than the stables) drifting in and out of sleep, dreaming about Roman maths tests. Just as the teacher was about to discover Oliver had got all the answers wrong, a whole army of Roman soldiers burst into the classroom with a giant lion on a lead. It seemed like a good time to wake up.

Owl was already wide awake, standing on one leg in front of the barred window.

"Good morning," he said cheerfully. "Just doing a spot of yoga – you know, balancing and stretching, that sort of thing. Very good for focusing the mind on the day ahead."

"I don't even want to *think* about the day ahead," replied Oliver, shivering. There was a knot in his stomach that had nothing to do with last night's dormice – it was today's lions that were the problem.

"Nonsense. We'll have you back at home eating apple pie before you know it. As soon as we take care of matters here…" Owl trailed off as a key turned in the lock. Their prison door swung open to reveal Dr Midnight himself, flanked by Gluteus and three mean-looking guards.

"Good morning, gentlemen," said Dr Midnight with a smile. It was his meanest, most evil smile yet, with bits of breakfast *and* yesterday's snail stuck between his teeth. "Lovely day for it, eh?"

"It certainly is." Owl swapped legs and smiled back to prove he wasn't scared, but Oliver's mouth was stuck tight with fear.

"There's going to be a big crowd at the games today," Dr Midnight went on. "It's always a good turnout when they bring in the wild animals. You'll be famous, the pair of you… at least until the lions gobble you up and spit out your bones."

Oliver covered his ears, trying to block out the words, but it was no good. He could still hear him.

"I'll be cheering you on, of course," said Dr Midnight, "unless I'm too busy counting up my money. It's not just bumper popcorn sales today, I'm charging everyone to use my Portaloo as well. Good thinking, eh?"

"Your Portaloo?" asked Owl, putting both feet back on the floor. He wasn't smiling any more, for some reason, and his face had gone deathly pale. "But… but… but I was hoping to use it before we went."

"Well you're too late," said Dr Midnight. "I had my men move it down to the amphitheatre first thing this morning. Don't worry, I've removed the time switch and added a coin slot and some extra loo roll. It's just a regular stinky old toilet now."

Owl looked more worried than ever.

"Yes, yes, I know what you're thinking," Dr Midnight went on. "The man's a genius. And you're quite right – that's *exactly* what I am. A downright evil genius who's about to make heaps of money while disposing of his silly, secret agent enemies at the same time. The perfect plan, I think you'll find. It can't fail. And in case you've got any bonkers ideas about escaping while I'm busy whipping my popcorn sales team into shape (a little bit of whipping never does these slaves any harm), then you'd better think again. I'm leaving you in the capable hands of my great-great-great-great-more-greats-than-I've-got-time-for-great-grandfather, Gluteus. He'll be escorting you to the amphitheatre in person."

Gluteus nodded and belched.

"Don't let them out of your sight, Gluteus," said Dr Midnight. "And no sneaking off to play with that ridiculous photo booth either. You can't possibly need any more pictures of yourself."

Gluteus's face fell.

"And," continued Dr Midnight, turning back to Owl, "I've permanently disabled the time function on the photo booth as well. There is, quite simply, no way out. You'll be spending the rest of your days right here in Roman Britain. Though, given your coming appointment with a big hungry lion, that shouldn't be too much of a problem for you!" And with that he swept out of the room, leaving Gluteus and the guards in charge. "Remember," he called back over his shoulder. "Don't let them out of your sight!"

Oliver badly wanted to talk to Owl. What was the problem with the Portaloo? Had that been part of his cunning plan? And where did the borrowed nappy pin come in? It wasn't really for his loincloth, was it? But Gluteus and the guards crowded into the small room with them, making talking impossible. There was nothing for it but to wait and see. Owl settled back against the wall with his eyes shut and a funny expression on his face.

"What are you doing?" barked Gluteus after a

few minutes.

"Just thinking," said Owl.

"Well don't. Dr Midnight didn't say anything about letting you think."

"Very well," said Owl. "And what do you propose we do instead?"

"I spy?" suggested one of the guards. "Go on, I love a game of I spy. I'll go first. I spy with my little eye, something beginning with 'w'."

"Window?" guessed Oliver.

"No. Guess again."

"Wall?" asked another guard.

"Got it! Okay, your turn."

"I spy with my little eye, something beginning with 'w'."

"Window?" tried Owl.

"Yes! How did you guess?"

"Because the only things in this room other than you ugly lot are four walls and a window. It is quite possibly the most boring room it has ever been my misfortune to stay in."

Gluteus looked hurt. "You might as well wait at the amphitheatre if you're going to be like that," he said. "Maybe you'll find the gladiators' quarters more to your liking."

The guards hauled the prisoners to their feet and dragged them back out of the villa into the daylight. Owl was still quiet but Oliver was relieved to see he was smiling again. Hopefully that meant he had a new plan up his sleeveless toga. A bigger and better one this time, though. One that might actually work…

They set off at a quick march towards the town, with Gluteus travelling alongside on a poor squashed-looking horse. Oliver knew the route well now, recognising the herds of sheep and pigs on their left, and the fields of wheat to the right. But the knot in his stomach tightened with every passing landmark… what if those were the last sheep he ever saw? The last river? The last trees? The last cemetery…? *No*, he told himself. *Don't think about graves. Think about something nice… like kittens.*

Think about cute fluffy kittens… only the kittens somehow turned into lions, and the knot in his stomach became a tangle of misery and fear. But on the plus side, at least his pants weren't falling down anymore.

The town felt different today, with a holiday sense of excitement about the place. It was probably a religious festival of some kind if there were games on at the amphitheatre, although Oliver had never felt less excited in his life. Terrified? Yes. Scared out of his mind? Definitely. But as they passed under the far gate and the towering round walls of the amphitheatre loomed into view, Oliver hunched his neck down into his shoulders, feeling as excited as a hedgehog on a motorway. A blind, three-legged hedgehog with no chance of escape…

The amphitheatre was already filling up by the time they arrived. Oliver stared helplessly through the entrance into the arena, with a sick feeling rising in his chest. Owl wasn't smiling any more either.

"Come on then," said Gluteus sharply. "The

sooner you're safely down in the gladiators' quarters, the better."

Owl shook his head. "Not yet. I need to use the toilet first."

"Oh no you don't. Dr Midnight didn't say anything about toilets."

Owl crossed his legs. "But I'm really, *really* desperate. Nerves do *terrible* things to my tummy. And I always get nervous before I'm torn to pieces by a lion. Come to think of it, I'm not sure last night's baked beans helped either."

"Erm…" Gluteus seemed to be wavering. "No, I don't think I can allow it. You'll just have to hold it in."

"Please," begged Owl, pulling a horrible face. "It feels like my stomach's about to explode any second now. Look," he said, pointing to Dr Midnight's Portaloo, with a long queue of people waiting to use it. "Let me pop in there… before it's too late. You can always tell those people to let me go first. I'm sure they'll listen to an important man like you."

Gluteus puffed his chest out. "Of course they will. I'm very well-respected in these parts, you know… Oh, alright," he finally agreed, "but you'd better make it quick." He pointed to two of his guards. "You wait right outside, do you understand? He mustn't get away. And as for you," he said to Oliver, "you're staying here with me where I can keep my eye on you."

"Thank you," said Owl, clutching dramatically at his stomach. "Don't worry," he whispered to Oliver under his breath, "I'll come back for you. I promise."

"Out of their way, out of their way!" shouted Gluteus as the guards pushed Owl to the front of the queue. "Prisoner coming through."

The guards hammered on the toilet door until a flustered red-faced man opened it.

"Alright, alright, keep your hair on," he began… then he caught sight of the big swords the guards were wielding. "Of course," he said, with a scared smile. "Be my guest, I'd just about finished anyway."

Owl reached for his hidden nappy pin and stepped inside, shutting the door behind him. Was this part of his cunning plan, Oliver wondered, or a sudden case of the tummy runs? Because what good was a time machine with no time function? But then, even as he stood there wondering, there was a loud whir and a bang, and the Portaloo vanished into thin air, leaving a queue of angry people crossing their legs. The big burly guards looked rather small and scared all of a sudden.

"Uh-oh," said the first one, pulling a face. "Dr Midnight won't be pleased when he finds out we've lost his prisoner *and* his favourite loo."

"Tell me about it," agreed the second. "You know what happened to the last fella who did that…"

CHAPTER XVII

"Neptune's nostril hair!" cried Gluteus, wringing his hands. "Vulcan's verruca! The prisoner's disappeared. Oh, this is bad. This is *very* bad."

The first guard began to cry as the queue of toilet-desperate people all started shouting at once.

Oliver, on the other hand, was feeling much more cheerful. Now that Owl had the time machine he'd be back to rescue him any moment now... Yes, any moment now... He stood there, poised for action, ready to jump in the moment the blue Portaloo reappeared. But nothing happened. No strange whirring sounds. No bangs. No sign of any loos whatsoever.

"You'll just have to hold it in a bit longer," the second guard told the angry queue. "I'm sure it'll be back soon."

But it wasn't. Oliver's hope turned to panic as the minutes ticked by. Where was Owl? Why hadn't he come back like he promised?

"Right then," said Gluteus at last. "I suppose one prisoner is better than none at all. Let's get you down to the gladiators' quarters before you disappear as well."

They marched Oliver down to a dark, dank room underneath the arena. The stale air was heavy with the smell of sweat and blood. Like Oliver's tunic, only worse.

"Urgghh," moaned one of the guards. "It's a bit whiffy down here."

"Enough of your cheek," said Gluteus. "Or I'll give you something *really* whiffy to moan about. You know what those beans do to me."

Oliver felt for the honey-coated dormice he'd tucked into his pocket to distract the lion with. *That* plan seemed more pathetic than ever in the cold light of day, but with Owl missing in action it was the only one he had. "What happens now?" he asked.

"We sit here and wait until it's your turn," said Gluteus, "and then we give you a nice sword and send you outside to play. Just you and the big furry kitty..." He pulled a collection of photos out of his toga and sat down in the corner to admire himself all over again. "Just look at those shapely shell-like ears. That wonderful rounded wart..."

Where, oh where, was Owl? Oliver paced up and down the room, listening to the gathering crowds above him – to the noise of clapping and cheering as the games got under way. Any minute now, he kept telling himself. Any minute now and Owl would be back for him.

The minutes came and went and still there was no sign of the Portaloo. Another bloodthirsty roar of delight spilled down from the arena, followed by a wild scream of pain.

"*Pssst*," came a hiss from nearby. A soft, secret

kind of hiss.

Oliver turned to see a funny-looking slave girl with badly cut hair and a fresh mud beard plastered to her chin.

"Jules! How did you get down here? Did Owl send you? Is he waiting outside?"

Jules shook her head. "No, I'm sorry. I haven't seen him since he whisked you away from school. And the only person waiting outside is a scary-looking guard with a sword. He didn't want to let me in at first – said they've already lost one of their prisoners and can't risk losing another – but I softened him up with that joke about the one-legged duck with a welly on his head, and he's given me two minutes to say my goodbyes." She sniffed, wiping away a tear with the back of her hand. "I heard there was a young boy fighting the lion today and I had a horrible feeling it might be you. So I made myself a new beard – just in case I bumped into my old master – and came as quickly as I could. And here you are." She dropped her voice to a whisper. "What are you going to do? Have you thought of a plan?"

"I don't know," said Oliver, bleakly. "Not unless you've got a stun gun tucked behind your back? Or a missing Portaloo?"

Jules wrinkled her nose. "I don't even know what a stun gun is. Or a porta-whats-it. I have brought you something though." She held out a misshapen wax blob threaded onto a loop of pink wool. "It's a bulla," she said. "For luck."

Oliver remembered seeing one at the museum – a sort of amulet with charms inside, given to Roman boys when they were nine days old to ward off evil spirits. Did they work on evil lions though? That was the question.

Jules looped it over his head, standing back to admire her handiwork. "Sorry, I didn't have any gold, or lead, only wax. And it might have melted a bit on the way here…"

"It's perfect," said Oliver, forcing a smile. "I feel luckier already. Thank you. How's everything going with Educo?" he asked, changing the subject.

"It's brilliant," Jules told him. "We started reading lessons last night. *And* we did some extra maths this morning even though it's a holiday. I've never been happier… at least I *was* happy until I heard about you and the lion…"

"Oi, you, funny beardy boy!" Gluteus waved a set of photos under Jules's nose. "Where did you come from? Are you the owly man's replacement?"

"No," said Oliver. "Definitely not. She just came to wish me luck for the fight. *He* came to wish me luck, I mean. You'd better get out of here," he added, turning back to Jules. "Thank you for my bulla. And thank you for making the last few minutes of my life a bit more…" But the end of his sentence was lost beneath a wild roar of applause above their heads.

"That's our cue," said Gluteus, shooing Jules out of the way. He grabbed hold of Oliver's shoulders and swung him back towards the tunnel. "Come on, you're up next. Time to go."

Oliver's stomach lurched. This couldn't be

happening. He must be dreaming. Yes, maybe the whole thing was one big nightmare and all he needed to do was wake up. He closed his eyes and pinched his arm, squeezing the skin between his fingers... Nothing. He pinched himself again, even harder. But when he opened his eyes he was still in the gladiators' quarters of a Roman amphitheatre, about to take on a hungry lion. Only now he had a sore arm as well.

One of the guards handed him a sword but it was so heavy Oliver could barely lift it. How was he supposed to fight a lion with *that*? He didn't have much choice though. The noise from the arena was getting louder all the time and there was still no sign of Owl. What was he playing at?

"Hurry up then," said Gluteus cheerfully, pushing Oliver up the tunnel. "They're waiting for you. Try and do a bit of running around first before the messy eating bit. The audience will like that."

Oliver stumbled out into the scorching sunshine, staggering sideways under the weight of the sword.

The wild clapping and cheering echoed around his skull, his head throbbing with the sudden noise and heat. *This can't be happening*, he told himself again, trying not to look at the drying bloodstains by his feet. *This can't be happening.* But it was. Purple spots danced in front of his eyes as he stood there blinking, wishing he still had his S Service sunglasses with him… wait, no he didn't… he wished he'd never even *heard* of Her Majesty's S Service.

The watching crowds didn't seem to have noticed he was only a schoolboy – the harder his legs trembled and shook, the louder they cheered. Or maybe they just didn't care. At that precise moment in time, Oliver would have given anything to be safely back at school where he belonged. In fact, he'd rather be anywhere else in the world, anywhere else in history, than standing on the edge of a blood-splattered dirt circle, waiting for the lion to arrive. If ever there was a good time for a Portaloo to appear out of nowhere, it was now.

There was a horrible roaring noise. Oliver froze. Even with the sun in his eyes there was no mistaking the huge lion-shaped figure on the far side of the arena. It stood there, growling, shaking its mane and pawing at the ground like a bull preparing to charge.

The crowd fell quiet as they waited for the fun to start. Everyone was watching now… watching and waiting. Oliver could see Dr Midnight in the front row, tossing popcorn into the air and catching it in his mouth. There was Eyebrow, dragging a young boy along the row of seats by his left ear. And there was the man from the fast food stall, waving a sausage at him for luck.

The lion roared again – even louder this time. Oliver summoned up all his strength and lifted his sword as high as he could. And then the lion charged. Oliver's heart was beating so fast it almost burst out of his chest as a blur of golden fur and hunger came hurtling towards him. Nearer and nearer. Before he knew it, the lion was just feet away.

Clang! Oliver's sword clattered, useless, to the ground. He started to reach for a dormouse but it was too late. There was the lion, with his cavernous red mouth and knife-like claws. Too late. Too late. Oliver shut his eyes and waited.

But the attack never came. There was a loud crackling sound where the lion's roar should have been… and then nothing. Oliver opened one eye and peeped out. The lion had stopped, mid-attack, his attention caught by a new arrival in the arena. By a big blue Portaloo.

"Run!" shouted Owl as the toilet door opened.

"Run!" screamed Jules, arms and legs flailing wildly as she tried to wrestle herself free from Gluteus's guards.

Run! Oliver told his poor shaking legs. He shot off like a rocket, muscles and lungs burning with the effort. The lion pawed at the ground, staring from Owl to Oliver and back again, as if he was trying to make up his mind. And then he decided. He tore off after Oliver, covering the ground in great leaps and bounds.

It was no good. The lion was too quick. There was no way Oliver could reach the Portaloo in time. He scrabbled inside his tunic for a dormouse and threw it as hard as he could but the lion took no notice. Why would he? Why stop for dry, leftover snacks when he had a fresh juicy meal just a few paces away?

Then, out of the corner of his eye, Oliver saw Owl reach back into the Portaloo. An arm shot out and something red and round came hurtling through the air towards them. *Smack!* A bowl of Josephine's dog food hit the lion square on the back of his head, sending him tottering sideways across the arena in a dizzy muddle of paws, mewling softly to himself like a kitten.

"Run!" shouted Owl a second time. Dr Midnight was on his feet now, screaming to his guards to catch them, while the crowds looked on in confusion. Some people were cheering, others were booing.

"Stop that boy!" yelled Dr Midnight. "Don't let

him get away!"

"Run!" shouted the man from the fast food stall, pelting the guards with spare sausages. "You can do it!"

Oliver was nearly there but the guards were right behind him now. With one giant leap, he flung himself in through the open door, just as Owl flicked his cunningly crafted nappy pin time switch and pressed the flush. There was a whir and a bang and the arena vanished.

CHAPTER XVIII

Oliver sank back onto the toilet seat as silvery purple clouds swirled around them.

Owl grinned. "Nice of you to drop in," he said. "Close the door behind you, though. We don't want anyone falling out."

"Where are we?" gasped Oliver, panting with relief as he reached out for the handle and tugged the door shut. The Portaloo stank but he didn't care.

"Somewhere in the mists of time," said Owl. "As for where we're going, only time will tell."

"What do you mean?"

"I didn't have a chance to set the controls properly," Owl explained. "We might be heading for the Stone Age, or we could be zooming our way into the future. Who knows? Let's face it, anywhere's got to be better than where we've just come from."

"I thought it was all over," said Oliver. "He was about to eat me."

"Yes, sorry about that," Owl apologised. "I came back as soon as I could but this nappy pin time switch is a bit unreliable."

"It was a good job you had that bowl of Josephine's dog food with you."

"Oh no," said Owl, "that wasn't Josephine's. I ended up in the twenty-sixth century, by mistake, getting chased by a mutant pet skunk. And when I ran off with his food, thinking it might be good to distract the lion with, he stink-sprayed me! Bleurgh! The sooner I get out of this toga and into a nice hot shower the better."

Oliver knew the feeling. "Is that where we're going now? Home?"

"Not just yet. We still have to get back to the time Dr Midnight first arrived and stop him changing history."

"And then everything will go back to how it was before?" asked Oliver, thinking about Jules. *"Everything?"*

Owl nodded. "It will be like none of us were ever here."

"I'll need to make a quick detour over to the West Gate, in that case, once we've taken care of Dr Midnight. There's someone I need to see…"

"Of course," said Owl, when Oliver explained his plan. "Hold on tight though, we'll be landing any minute n–"

Oof!

The Portaloo landed with a bump and Oliver slipped off the toilet, banging his elbow on the wall.

"Would you mind sticking your head out and seeing where we are," asked Owl, "while I have a go at fixing this time switch?"

Oliver squeezed past him and opened the door. They were in the middle of a dense forest, with giant birds flying overhead.

"Woah!" he cried. "Look at the size of them!"

He was just wishing he had his camera with him when one of the birds came swooping down towards the Portaloo. The closer it flew the more exotic it looked, with its long beak and huge leathery wings. Oliver had never seen a bird like it. And then he realised why. It wasn't a bird at all – it was a pterodactyl.

"Woah," he said again, slamming the door shut as quickly as he could. "I think we're a bit on the early side," he told Owl.

"Okay then." Owl gave the nappy pin a final tweak and re-flushed the chain. "Let's see if that's done the trick."

The Portaloo lurched to one side and they were off again. Oliver settled back down on the toilet with a smile. Perhaps being a secret agent wasn't so bad after all… apart from being chased and captured and almost turned into lion lunch. The food wasn't exactly great either, but getting to see real-life dinosaurs from the safety of a time machine was *so* much better than reading about them at school.

The Portaloo stopped a second time and he peered out. They seemed to have landed slap bang in the middle of a round theatre, next to a funny-looking man in ladies' tights. Perhaps *he* was having an embarrassing underwear day as well.

"To be, or not to be, that *was* the question," said the man, staring in wide-eyed wonder at the Portaloo. "But all is forgot at the sight of this wondrous blue beast and its blood-stained master. Tell me," he said to Oliver, "what art thou?"

"I'm er… Oliver. A traveller from the land of Futuria."

The man rubbed his eyes. "Is't possible? Do I dream?"

"Yes, that's right," said Oliver. "This is all just a dream. You should be waking up any minute now… I think we're in the middle of a Shakespeare play or something," he whispered to Owl. "We need to go back a bit further."

"Okay," said Owl. "I'll try again. Quick, close

the door."

Oliver bowed low to the audience and pulled the door shut. The Portaloo shot back off through the silvery purple mist.

"Right. I think I've cracked it now," said Owl as they landed with another bump. "And I've reset the co-ordinates so we should end up back at Gluteus's villa. Let's have a look."

CHAPTER XIX

"Well we're in the right place," said Oliver, opening the door again. There was Gluteus's toilet and his disgusting sponge on a stick. "But are we in the right time?"

"Shh," whispered Owl. "I can hear voices…"

"What kind of strange message?" they heard Gluteus ask.

"It's to do with one of your relatives," answered a second voice. "A *distant* relative. Some kind of doctor, I think. According to the oracle, he'll be here at midday and he's bringing his pet dog with him."

"But there aren't any doctors in my family." That was Gluteus again. "And I don't like dogs. Why is he coming *here*?"

"I don't know," said the second voice. "The oracle didn't say."

Gluteus let out a big sigh. "Well, we'll find out soon enough I suppose. It's almost midday now."

The voices died away and Owl flashed Oliver a smug grin.

"Perfect," he said. "Right time, right place. I'm not just a pretty face, eh?"

"Absolutely not," agreed Oliver. Not even Owl's mother could accuse him of having one of those.

"So all we have to do now is wait," said Owl, taking up his position. "Don't panic if *our* Portaloo disappears for a bit. That's a good sign. It means Dr Midnight's one is on its way. According to the rules of time travel they can't both exist at the same time."

Oliver nodded as if it all made perfect sense, although his brain ached just thinking about it. He gave his wax bulla a quick rub for extra luck, before that disappeared too, and took his place on the other side of the door, poised for action. A few minutes later the Portaloo vanished for a whole five seconds and then reappeared, like a magic trick. Oliver held his breath as the door opened…

Out stepped Dr Midnight, sizing up the Roman toilets like a holidaymaker just arrived at his new hotel. *POW!* That was the end of his holiday though, thanks to Owl's super-fast karate chop. There were no burly guards or old ladies around to help their master either – they hadn't been recruited yet. Dr Midnight teetered on the spot for a moment, wobbling on his feet before crashing to the ground, unconscious. One down, one to go.

Josephine growled, fangs bared as she leapt off the toilet seat, heading for Oliver's ankles, but he was ready for her this time. He took a honey-coated dormouse from his tunic and flung it across the room. The poodle tore after it, barking wildly.

"Quick," ordered Owl. "Grab that loo roll while she's distracted, and let's get wrapping."

Round and round Oliver went with the toilet roll, binding Dr Midnight's arms tight into his sides like an Egyptian mummy. They'd seen one of those on their school trip to the museum too, and a mummified cat Florence had nicknamed 'Tutankhamoggy'.

"Now for that pesky dog," said Owl, once they'd bundled Mummy Midnight into the Portaloo, wedging him in between the seat and the ceiling.

What? Oliver gulped. Surely they weren't going to tie *Josephine* up with loo roll? She'd bite straight through it in a second, and then she'd start on their fingers. No, he had a much better idea.

He ducked around the back of the Portaloo and removed his knicker nappy pin. Mrs Starling's royal pants came sliding down around his ankles and he kicked them off over his sandals. There! They might be the most embarrassing frilly mistake in the history of underwear mistakes, but they'd make the perfect poodle-catcher.

"Sorry, your Majesty," he muttered, as the Queen's heads stared back at him disapprovingly. "But this is an emergency."

Oliver edged towards the snarling dog with his poodle-catcher at the ready.

Owl seemed surprised at first – "where did *those* come from? Is that my good friend Her Majesty on the back?" – but once Oliver explained his plan he put his fingers to his mouth and let out a long hooting whistle.

"Josephine," Owl called. "Oh, Josephine! Come here, you horrible yappy little bundle of fur and teeth. We've got another mouse treat for you."

Josephine looked up and snarled as Oliver dropped the last remaining dormouse at his feet.

"Come and get it!" he called.

The poodle came charging back towards him, mouth open and eyes blazing. She pounced on the mouse with a ferocious growl, just as Oliver pounced on her with a frilly snap of elastic. She didn't seem *quite* so scary anymore – not compared to the lion – but her teeth looked as sharp as ever. He worked quickly, while her mouth was too busy eating to bite, bundling her front legs through one hole and her back legs through the other. And then he scooped her up by the waistband like a wriggling, snarling handbag, adding a nappy pin handle at the top to dangle off the toilet roll hook inside the Portaloo. Hopefully it would hold until they got back to S Service HQ.

"And now for one last trip into town," announced Owl, readjusting the co-ordinates. "Just by the West Gate, did you say?"

"Yes, that's right." Oliver squeezed himself into the corner away from Josephine's mouth, and got ready for take-off. One last trip and then home!

"*Pssst*," Oliver hissed. A soft, secret kind of hiss.

The long-haired, clean-chinned slave girl looked up in surprise.

"Huh?" Her nose wrinkled as she stared back at Oliver in confusion. "Do I know you?"

"No," said Oliver, "but I know you. I know your

name's Jules – Julia – and I know you hate working for your master. I know that you dream of running away and joining the army – but deep down what you *really* want to do, more than anything else, is to go to school. Because as well as being brave and determined and kind, you're also brilliant at sums."

"W…w… what? How could you possibly know all that?"

"It's hard to explain," said Oliver. "Let's just say if things were different I know we'd be friends. That's why I want you to have this." He handed over Owl's bag of coins – the one Agent B had given him back at S Service HQ. "It's to buy your freedom with. And then you need to find Educo Constantis, the teacher, and offer to help with the cooking and cleaning in return for board and lessons. He might take a bit of convincing but be sure to mention how good your honey cakes and barley soup are. That should do the trick."

"But… but…"

"Trust me," said Oliver. "Just do as I say and

you'll be happier than you've ever been before."

"Hurry up," said Owl, leaning out of the Portaloo door. "Dr Midnight's starting to come round."

"I've got to go," Oliver told her. "Good luck. Be brilliant."

"Thank you," said Jules, staring down at the purse in her hand as if she couldn't believe it was real. "Wait, you haven't even told me your name."

"Oliver," he called back over his shoulder. "My name's Oliver." And with that he took one last look at Roman Britain – at the greatest adventure of his life – and stepped inside the crowded Portaloo.

"I'm ready now," he told Owl. "Let's go."

CHAPTER XX

"Ooohhrhrr," groaned Dr Midnight as they finally landed. "Where am I?"

"Back at S Service HQ, hopefully," said Owl. "And if my calculations are correct it should be Thursday lunchtime – only a couple of hours after we left. Which is good news for us, Oliver, because it's toad-in-the-hole on Thursdays. I *much* prefer toads to mice and snails, don't you?"

Oliver's stomach rumbled. He wasn't just hungry, he was ravenous. After all, he hadn't eaten in *centuries*.

The Portaloo door swung open to a huge round of applause. All the other agents had gathered round to welcome them back.

"Well done, Agent Starling," said Agent B, as Oliver handed over the growling poodle pants. "Oh my, what an interesting dog-catcher – I love those pink frills!"

"I'll need it back once you've finished with it, I'm afraid," said Oliver. "It doesn't really belong to me... Speaking of which, I don't suppose you've got any spare S Service underwear I could borrow?"

"Secret pants?" said Agent B. "Why of course, dear boy. I'll have Neeta send down a pair of our new propel-o-pants for you to try. Mind how you go with them though. Whatever you do, *don't* pull the red ribbon on the side... unless you like being jet propelled through the air at sixty miles an hour!"

Owl followed Oliver out of the Portaloo, leaving Gorilla to take care of the evil genius loo roll mummy that was Dr Midnight. Norman was waiting for him with a brand-new pair of S Service dark glasses.

"Oh yes," said Owl, putting them on with a

satisfied sigh. "That's better. All I need now is my trusty beard and raincoat and I'll be a happy man."

Oliver stretched his trousered legs out under the table. It felt great to be back in his own clothes again – apart from the propel-o-pants, of course. If only he'd been wearing *them* when that lion was chasing after him.

"What happens now?" he asked, having polished off his third helping of toad-in-the-hole, with extra mashed potato.

"The police will take Dr Midnight off to a top-secret, top-security jail," said Owl, wiping gravy off his fake beard, "while I finish up the last of this sausage."

"And Josephine will be taken to his mum's house," added Agent B. "Mrs Midnight usually looks after his dog for him until his next escape."

"What do you mean?" asked Oliver. "How do

you know he'll escape?"

"Because, dear boy, he's an evil genius. That's his job. And it's our job to catch him again when he does."

"Oh, I see," said Oliver. "And what about me?"

Agent B smiled. "You must be keen to get home."

"Yes, of course I am, only…"

"Only what?"

"You said we wouldn't get back until *after* the maths test, but that's tomorrow. And I already did a test, yesterday, back in Roman times… Or was that today…?" Oliver's head hurt just thinking about it. Time travel could be very confusing.

"Don't worry," said Agent B, "that's all taken care of." He reached inside his pocket and handed Oliver a telegram from the Queen. "Her Majesty excuses you from all tests tomorrow in recognition of your services to the country. Better than a sick note, eh?"

Oliver grinned. *Neptune's nostril hair!* Just wait

until he showed his mum. She'd be baking celebration apple pies for the next year!

"And you might want to hold on to this," said Owl, handing Oliver his mini Roman Britain book. "I think you'll find history is back to normal, thanks to us. No more popcorn and Burger Emperor baked beans. No more nappy-pinned togas and birthday badges. And your great-great-great-great-more-greats-than-we've-got-time-for-great-grandfather Titus Stabbicus is back to being a famous centurion again. We did it, Oliver. We saved history." Owl winked. "Although you might want to have a look at the very last page…"

Not Emperor Midnight, surely? Oliver flicked to the back of the book and grinned. No, it wasn't the world's number one evil genius emperor, it was a picture of a familiar-looking Roman woman called Julia, famed throughout the Empire for her mathematical skills and fondness for mud beards. There was another picture underneath, of a stone tablet recently discovered by archaeologists in the foundations of her old Roman schoolroom.

"What does that say?" Oliver asked, squinting at the faded inscription.

"Hmm," said Agent B. "My Latin's a bit rusty but I'd take a guess at THANK YOU OLIVER."

Owl wasn't the only one snoring on the way back home. Oliver woke with a start as they turned into Sherlock Avenue, to see Mrs Peeker's net curtains twitching like crazy.

"It's Oliver," called Mr Starling, throwing open the front door. "He's home. I wonder if he's…"

"It's Oliver!" shouted his wife, running out onto the rain-splashed pavement, too excited to listen to her husband. Oliver was embarrassed to see she was still wearing the tiara and bunting. "He's home!"

Mrs Starling threw her arms around her son as he got out of the car, squeezing him tight.

"Let me look at you," she said at last, stepping

back. "Oh Oliver, you've got gravy all round your mouth. Here, let me wipe that off…" She reached in her pocket for a tissue and spat on it.

"One moment, madame," said Owl, handing her his tiny secret agent mobile phone. "There's an important call for you."

"Hello," she said, in her best telephone voice. "Mrs Eleanor Starling speaking." There was a long pause. "I'm sorry, *who* did you say? The *Queen*…? As in 'God Save Our Gracious Queen'? As in 'send her victorious, happy and glorious'?"

Mrs Starling knelt down on the pavement, in what turned out to be a rather large puddle, and bowed her head.

"Oh your Majesty," she whispered. "You don't know what an honour this is. May I just say…" But that was as far as she got.

"Hello?" came a small voice from the other end of the phone. "Hello, are you still there? Oh dear, I think the corgis have been chewing the phone line again. Can you hear me?"

But Mrs Starling didn't reply.

"She must have fainted," said Oliver's dad, scooping her up out of the puddle.

"Or perhaps she fainted," echoed the Queen.

"That's what *I* said," grumbled Mr Starling.

Ah yes, thought Oliver, grinning at Owl and waving across the road to Mrs Peeker. It was good to be home.